First Printing Lock 'n Load Publishing Paperback Edition 2019
Copyright © 2019 Lock 'n Load Publishing, LLC.
All Rights Reserved.
Printed in the United States of America in the State of Colorado
Lock 'n Load Publishing LLC
1027 North Market Plaza, Suite 107 - 146
Pueblo West, Colorado, 81007
Rev 13
ISBN: 9-781733-104128

CONTENTS

INTRODUCTION

"The Ghost Insurgency" is set in Keith Tracton's "World at War '85" game series from Lock 'n Load Publishing. You don't have to play the game to enjoy this novel but it's definitely worth checking out if you are one of those people who enjoys having fun. The events that happen herein are a tiny microcosm of that splendid universe but they are no less important than the tank battles that raged in the Fulda Gap or the air war conducted in the skies near Hannover. This story is a little different than the straight-up war stories in the series – it pries up the dark frayed edges of the war and examines the covert battles that were fought in the shadows.

If you haven't read any of the other books in this series so far, don't worry. They are mostly self-contained tales that can be enjoyed without knowing any of the backstory. All you really need to know is that it is May 1985 and war has broken out between the Warsaw Pact and NATO. Of course, if you have read the other books, you'll notice a recurring character from First Strike (that's CIA operative David Heath if you're dying to find out) and mention of major events such as the war's origins and its general progress.

"The Ghost Insurgency" is a much more personal story than the others. Instead of looking at military tactics and hardware, this one is about human beings and the effect of combat and trauma on the individual.

It is also about exploring the legacy of the Vietnam war, which Americans were just starting to come to grips with around the time this novel was set. After a long period in which the war (and sadly, its participants) were ignored by society and the wider culture, the 1980s saw a gradual willingness to look back at what happened and how it affected the men who returned home. This was evident in American pop culture at the time – movies such as Platoon and Full Metal Jacket were huge hits with audiences while TV heroes like Magnum P.I. had a Vietnam war backstory that played a serious and prominent part in the character's outlook and development.

"The Ghost Insurgency" sits at the intersection of Vietnam and "World at War '85". In almost every way imaginable, the American military of the immediate post-Vietnam War years was different than that of the mid-1980s. Rebuilt from the ashes, the latter was disciplined, well-trained, and equipped with the latest technology. It was also staffed with people who had learned the hard lessons of war and knew how to apply them. Many of the enlistees and junior officers who served in the US Army during that time were raised under the tutelage of Vietnam veterans who vowed never again to repeat the experiences that shaped their own youth. This book's main character, Joe Ricci, is one of those very men.

Thanks for reading

Sincerely,
Brad Smith
April 2019

ACKNOWLEDGMENTS

"The Ghost Insurgency" owes its life to an obscure book called "Improvised Radio Jamming Techniques: Electronic Guerrilla Warfare" by Lawrence K. Myers (Paladin Press, 1989). This is a lengthy manual written for SF operators and it is a fascinating read if you can find it. The book details methods and principles of radio jamming and interception. It also cites historical uses of these techniques in recent conflicts such as Vietnam.

Joe Ricci's mention of the NVA's dedicated deception units used to call in American artillery fire on US troops is historically accurate. In 1969, the 25th Infantry Division conducted a raid near Saigon that located a vast underground complex dedicated solely to this task. The enemy prisoners were found to speak flawless English and were trained at breaking all manner of American codes.

The incident described at Sperenberg is based on some speculation in the book about a real-world event that may have been caused by radio deception. Myers hints that the 1988 death of President Zia of Pakistan may have been due to an operation that transmitted false radio signals to the aircraft. I have no idea if this is true or not, but it certainly took the exploits of Joe Ricci and Ned Littlejohn in an interesting direction.

This book could not have happened without the support of my family. My wife and son both gave me the strength to pursue the path of the writer and forego the certainty of a steady paycheck. As luck would have it, I ended up having something to say after all. Thanks to the readers who have supported the books so far and enjoy them despite (or even because) of their flaws. Each novel gets me a little closer to "getting it right" but I admittedly still have a long way to go.

Last but not least, I owe a debt of gratitude to David Heath, Preston Rosales, Marc von Martial, Blackwell Hird, and the many others at Lock 'n Load Publishing who stood behind my work and had the confidence to ask for more. If you keep asking for it, I'll certainly continue writing.

THE GHOST INSURGENCY

BRAD SMITH

PURSUIT

Captain Joe Ricci shielded his eyes against the glare of the mid-morning sun and scanned the thick hilly forests to the east. The broad leaves and branches of the tall cypress trees were stirred only by the soft ripples of a hot breeze. With no visible sign of his pursuers, he turned again to the business of trudging up the unforgiving slope that led back home.

Each ragged step sent stabs of agony shuddering along his calves. Like a drunk leaving a bar, he weaved on unsteady legs over the smooth rocky face on his way to the summit. A look up ahead revealed the Hmong fighters with him were just as tired. Running up and down the rugged terrain all night had brought all of them to the breaking point. Now they gasped and grunted as they paced upward like automatons focused only on ceaseless forward motion.

Ricci's vision blurred for a moment as he tried not to think about how much longer this uphill torture would continue. Twenty strides? Thirty? It didn't matter. One careful step at a time, he would make it back to the little village where he and his men lived and trained.

Up ahead, someone stumbled to the ground and did not move.

Ricci scrambled up the bald rocky surface to where one of the Hmong fighters lay. The man threw up an arm as if he were drowning. Ricci grabbed it and let the man's reedy fingers dig into his wrist. Half-lidded eyes veered toward the summit and then stared back at him like an accusation. Ricci threw all his energy into a faint smile.

"Let's go," he creaked.

The Hmong fighter picked up a foot and aimed his body towards the summit. Ricci came staggering up behind him, fending off collapse the entire way.

When all twelve men crested the hill, there was no celebration. They simply fell in a heap on the hard earth. Some guys retched. Ricci did too.

Scott Baker crawled over and yanked on Ricci's sleeve. Six foot three inches and thick as a firefighter, the lieutenant was Ricci's second-in-command. He wasn't the captain's first choice to be out here in the field. There were four others in the A-Team detachment with better instincts for bush fighting. Those men were all back at base camp, training another group of Hmong to fight back against the communists who threatened their autonomy.

"Let's rest," said Baker.

Ricci looked around the bare circle of land that capped the hill. If the enemy charged up here, there would be no cover. Even a single well-placed mortar round could take half of them out. Staying here for any length of time was a dangerous gamble.

"Now?!" asked Ricci. "Here?!"

"I don't see any NVA behind us."

"Doesn't mean they aren't out there."

"We gotta stop. I know we're almost home but...we can't keep this up anymore."

The man had a point.

Three nights of sleep had been denied to them as the North Vietnamese Army hounded them, intent on revenge for the week-long series of ambushes that Ricci and the Hmong fighters had set upon the Ho Chi Minh Trail. Once in a while, the enemy would take potshots in the darkness, hoping the Hmong would fire back and reveal their position.

No one had taken the bait and Ricci was proud of them. Now finally, it seemed the Vietnamese had either gone back home or at least had taken a break from the chase. Ricci weighed his options. The going would be easier downhill. Any textbook would have told him to take heart in that alone and get the men moving. On the other hand, the heavy numbness in his limbs were enough to convince him to take a small rest.

"Sixty seconds," blurted out Ricci. "You just spent ten of them begging."

Baker grimaced and shook his head. "Remind me to frag you when we get back to Ban Ngoc."

When time was up, they got moving again. Each man groaned as they got to their feet and resumed the last leg of their journey.

Twenty minutes later, the band of fighters waded down into the valley. During the descent, the rocky terrain softened to form rice paddies dotted here and there with thick vegetation. Ricci spotted a familiar clump of trees off to the northwest and smiled.

When he directed the men towards it, Baker squeezed out a delirious little laugh.

"I thought you wanted to go home."

"I do," said Ricci. "But they might still be following us. We need to stop and check. Besides, I thought you wanted a rest."

"Fine. You brought a bulldozer to clear a path in there?"

Ricci sighed. "Listen, Scooter. I've been thinkin'…Heath told me there's a desk job open in Bangkok pushing paper in some air-conditioned office. Just say the word when we get back and I'll vouch for you -."

Baker rolled his eyes and gestured like a maitre'd at a fancy French restaurant. "Ohhh-kay! Fine. Après vous, m'sieur."

The Hmong fighters slid their small frames through the narrow gaps between the trees. Accustomed to the rugged landscape, their bodies navigated the thorny brambles of elephant grass. Ricci and Baker took a little longer as they dug the leafy hooks out from their skin. There was a reason it was called "wait a minute" grass.

Finally, they reached a break in the undergrowth that led to a small clearing. Ricci called a halt and watched as the Hmong sat down in silence and ate the last of the salted pork and rice.

Baker flopped to the ground and waved a hand around.

"You been here before?" he asked.

Ricci shrugged. "Yep. Ned found it. Showed it to me a few months ago when we were setting up counter-ambushes against the Pathet Lao. Good concealment."

Of the six-man Special Forces detachment that lived with and trained the Hmong fighters, Sergeant Ned Littlejohn was the scout of the group. The Indian was wiry like a TV antenna, and never uttered more words than needed to be said.

Deep into his second tour, Ned was a natural fighter who could sniff out a trail in the jungle and direct the team's efforts while keeping them safe from ambush. Over the long months they had served together, Ricci had formed a bond with the guy despite - or maybe because of - their disparate personalities.

Baker's eyes closed and a buzzing snore tore out of his mouth. The fatigue seeped back into Ricci's muscles, and the urge to doze nearly overwhelmed the Special Forces captain. He stood up and slapped his cheeks, conjuring to mind the laundry list of things that needed to be done.

At the top of it was a quick inspection to see what supplies were left. Ricci wasn't even sure if they had enough food and water to wander around the bush for another day. If they got into a firefight - well, he was down to two magazines and a grenade. The others couldn't have been doing much better.

In the center of the clearing were a dozen burlap bags laid out neatly on the moss-covered ground. He pulled out what was left of the ammunition and claymore mines and distributed them into twelve even piles. When the group had set out from Ban Ngoc a week ago, each fighter carried a thousand rounds and three claymores apiece. A quick count of the remainder amounted to around a hundred rounds for each man and two mines total.

Ricci pointed at the ground and looked over at Kai, the old man of the group.

"Not much left."

"Careful," said the old man.

"Right. Let's be careful with what we have here."

By god, the ammo was critically low! Ricci chastised himself for pushing things too far this time. His mode of operations was simple enough - he took a page right out of the Viet Cong playbook and conducted a guerrilla war against the communists in their own backyard.

Each time he went out in the field, he kept stringing along ambushes for the enemy to fall into. But this time, they had laid one trap too many and now their supplies were nearly gone. Ricci sighed and shook his head.

"We killed many," said Kai. "Many." The old man gave a toothless smile and patted Ricci's shoulder.

"Tell your men they did a good job."

"Yes. Good job."

It was true enough.

The leaves near the edge of the camp rustled and Ricci's hand shot out towards his M16 rifle. Before he could shoulder the weapon, the figure stepped into the light. It was Chee. The kid had followed them all the way from Ban Ngoc without an invitation or even asking for Ricci's okay.

Despite his youth and inexperience, the other fighters had accepted him immediately. Ricci had ordered him to stay out of the way and learn the basics of setting up ambushes, fire discipline, and weapon maintenance. Chee had done it all without complaint. After exchanging a few quiet words with Kai, the old man gestured to the kid.

"He says someone there. The hill."

"Hill?"

"Maybe NVA."

Ricci wracked his brains for the possibilities. He had just enough ammunition for a hasty ambush. If they hit the NVA with enough force, the survivors would have no choice but to break off and run for home. That would mean clear sailing all the way to back Ban Ngoc. Or they could keep running and hope to shake their pursuers. It would all depend on how many bad guys were out there. He needed more information before he could decide either way.

He pushed down the little stab of panic and turned to Kai.

"Lunch is over. Get everyone's butts into gear and get ready to go."

Kai clicked his tongue twice. The men scrambled for their weapons and sought cover amidst the rocks and tree stumps. Ricci gestured for Chee to lead him to his vantage point. The kid nodded and stepped through the break in the treeline. As they crawled through the tall untamed grass, Ricci mulled through his options.

If someone was indeed out there, they couldn't risk going back to Ban Ngoc today. If the NVA found the base of operations, they might send in men and tanks to destroy them all. On the other hand, it was possible that Chee was seeing things.

More than once, fatigue had played tricks with his own mind out here. It was so easy to mistake a bush for a sniper lying in wait. With exhaustion clouding the brain, a tree turned into an enemy soldier with a gun raised and ready to fire. What sounded like men talking in whispers usually turned out to be bird chatter.

Ricci scanned the hills and soaked in the view. The crown of mist near the summits had lifted like a curtain to reveal an unblemished blanket of natural beauty. The jungle's leafy extensions swayed along with the wind's gentle tides. There were no campfires. No calls or whistles blasted out between search teams. Best of all, no one shot at him. The tell-tale signs of human activity were absent.

Ricci turned to Chee and shrugged.

"Where?"

The kid jabbed a finger and made a sound that held no meaning. What was he trying to say? With the only semi-fluent English speaker of the bunch separated by two hundred meters of thick jungle, Ricci dismissed the idea of going back to fetch Kai.

"Slow down," he said. He waved his palm at the ground, hoping Chee would get the message and find the word he needed.

It never came. Chee peered through the foliage again and squinted. Ricci followed his gaze with a pair of binoculars. He was pointing at a clump of boulders near the top of the highest hill in the vicinity. The stony escarpment that swept down from it held a hundred crevices to hide in. If someone was up there, they had chosen some prime real estate for concealment. The jagged nature of the terrain could also have led an overactive mind to believe they saw something that simply wasn't there.

They spent ten minutes observing the hill and looking for any sign of movement. Nothing budged. Ricci's doubts were confirmed when he looked at Chee, who offered only a smiling shrug in reply. He was tempted to just pack up and go. They were all on their last legs and needed to get home.

Several of the men had wounds that needed to be looked at and cleaned up. There was no time to run around in the bush, chasing after ghosts. Still, there was always the chance he was wrong. It was worth at least a token effort to investigate.

When he returned to the clearing, Ricci jabbed a finger at Baker, Kai, and two others. Together with Chee, they staggered up the hillside to look for any signs of life. Poking around the rocks with their rifles at the ready, they encountered nothing but gnarled scrub and blankets of moss.

"We don't have time for this," said Baker.

Ricci pointed over at Chee. "He said he saw someone. We need to check it out."

"And you listened to a fifteen-year old greenie," said Baker. "Joe, I got a bridge back home I wanna sell you. Real cheap too."

Baker was right. They were wasting time up here. Each time Chee was asked to point out the precise location of the NVA, he changed his answer. After trudging around for a half hour and finding nothing amiss, Ricci gave up and headed back to the makeshift camp down in the valley.

"All right," he announced. "That settles it. We're going straight home."

Twenty minutes later, they were back in Ban Ngoc. The wives ran up to greet their exhausted husbands. Ricci settled down for a smoke with Ned Littlejohn while Baker sacked out in one of the mud huts that dotted the little village. Before Ricci could put away his lighter, Big Al wandered over and plopped his massive frame on a nearby stump.

"Heath wants to talk to you," he said. "He's on the radio. Needs you out there again real soon."

Ricci nodded and put the cigarette back to his lips. The CIA area officer was full of ideas about how to stick it to the NVA, which kept men like Ricci and the others very busy.

Since Laos was officially out of bounds for the United States military, it was Heath's show to run how he pleased. The Special Forces operated under the guise of advisers to civilians, which put them in a gray area between military and civilian operations.

The details were messy and Ricci didn't really understand them all - but it was all about politics; plausible deniability and avoiding the reach of an oversight committee. In truth, Laos was just part of the widening war in Southeast Asia that went on year after year with little to show for it all. Two years ago, Ricci had believed in what he was doing. Now, he wasn't so sure. Looking around, he couldn't see how the lives of anyone in this tiny village had improved since his arrival.

He looked over at Ned as the Marlboro burned down to the filter. Suddenly, the image of Brando cruising around on his motorcycle held a distinct and uncanny appeal. There was a better life waiting for him out there somewhere. It certainly wasn't here. Maybe it was as easy as just walking away.

"What do you figure, Ned? How about we just blow this joint instead?"

Littlejohn said nothing. His gaze was fixed on the tree line three hundred meters south. When he finally turned to Joe, his face was drawn and pale. A crease of worry took form over his narrow eyebrows.

"Joe," he said. "Someone's out there."

ABANDONMENT

Ban Ngoc, Laos
Approx. 15 miles west of the border with South Vietnam
July 12, 1970

The butt of the M16 bit hard into Joe Ricci's shoulder as he squeezed the trigger. A tinny bark echoed through the mud hut and the tan-uniformed man dropped to the bare floor. There was no time to gloat over the death of the NVA soldier. Judging from the clatter of the automatic weapons fire beyond the paper-thin walls, more enemies were out there waiting for him - many more. Ricci took hasty half-breaths and fumbled to insert the fresh magazine into the rifle.

"Dammit," he murmured. "They're here already."

Ricci slapped the bolt release and swept up his portable radio from the table. An explosion shook the walls as he stepped over the dying man's body and pushed open the bamboo door. He braced himself for what lay in wait on the other side.

The NVA were here in this Laotian village he had called home for the last six months, destroying everything in their path. From the mounting sound of enemy gunfire, it was clear enough what was happening - the simple inhabitants whom he and his Special Forces A-Team had fought and died with were being slaughtered.

Over on the other side of the border in South Vietnam, the American military fought against an invisible enemy that hit fast and disappeared into the jungles. Here in Laos, the roles were reversed. His current crop of American-led Hmong villagers were a small but agile strike team that laid careful traps for the North Vietnamese Army as they moved south along the Ho Chi Minh Trail.

Targets were selected by the CIA Area Chief David Heath and passed along to the local military commanders. As part of a covert war conducted without any real knowledge by the public, the rules were very simple - there were none. Ricci's men and the other A-Teams in the area had wreaked havoc on the North Vietnamese. Now they were here for revenge and things didn't look good.

Ricci stepped outside into the center of Ban Ngoc. The collection of simple homes made of mud and rock had a population of about 150 Hmong villagers. The place had been here for thousands of years, but at this rate, it wouldn't last another day.

On any given day of its existence, the village was filled with men and women and children leading simple rustic lives that centered around farming rice and raising families. Today, however, its inhabitants screamed in terror as their loved ones were cut down by gunfire and mortar rounds.

The mid-day heat hit Ricci like a slap in the face. The twin jet engines of a low-flying F-4 Phantom thundered overhead, ripping the leaves from the roof behind him. Small men in oversized US Army fatigues fired wildly into the dense jungle growth that grew on the hills that surrounded the village. The thrum of a Huey's blades dissipated as it disappeared over the spiky mountain ridges to the north.

If he had an idea of what was out there and where, he could call in an air strike and hit the enemy as hard as he could. One man in the whole village might know enough about the enemy's position for that. Ned Littlejohn had been out all morning among the hills and knew the best approaches to Ban Ngoc. Finding him might be the key to saving this place.

Ricci grabbed one of the Hmong fighters by the collar and screamed in his face. "Ned! Where's Ned?" Spittle from Ricci's mouth landed on the man's drab collar.

Terrified, the diminutive fighter shook his head to either side. Gibberish spilled out of his mouth.

Ricci's grip relaxed and he stalked around the corner of the nearest mud hut just in time to see four figures in pith helmets rush into the village. They stopped and stood in the center of it, spraying automatic fire from their Chinese-made Type 56 assault rifles.

Ricci dived for the cover of a muddy berm and watched in horror as Kai strode out from his home and crouched directly in front of the NVA. Bullets ripped all around the old man, striking the dirt and raising little fountains of scattered earth.

Amid the hail of death, Kai lifted his rifle with a calm determined slowness and took careful aim. Before he could shoot, one of the NVA rifles found its mark. The old man's head snapped back and he crumpled to the ground. Ricci shoved down the grief and anger. How could he have been so reckless? But there was no time to consider it. Of considerably more importance was the fact that the NVA were here now in groups. The perimeter was failing. Time was running out for Ban Ngoc.

"Breach!" Ricci screamed to no one. "They're coming through!"

The ground under the enemy fighters erupted in a column of dark smoke. When the dust settled, they were little more than a clump of corpses. Ricci's head swiveled, searching for whoever had fired off the claymores. Standing not fifty meters away amid a cluster of foxholes, was Ned Littlejohn, holding a detonator in his hand.

Ricci ran towards him, hollering in crazy adrenaline-fueled syllables. The blast of a mortar rang out somewhere behind him and he slid at the ground like he was running for first base on a single. A shower of pebbles rained over him as he caught his breath and counted his blessings.

For Ricci, it was yet another near miss in a war full of them. He got up and sprinted the remaining distance towards his friend, who reloading an SVD sniper rifle. Thick yellow tracers whizzed just above his head like angry insects.

When Ricci reached the foxhole, he wasted no more time in the crossfire - he jumped headfirst inside. The top of his skull banged painfully on the packed earth at the bottom of the defensive position.

After a few seconds of flailing, he stood shoulder-to-shoulder with his best friend.

Ned Littlejohn lifted the sniper's scope to eye-level and fired. The report was so loud that Ricci's ears rang and his head pounded. A hail of return fire forced him to duck back down into the foxhole. When at last it slackened, he nudged Littlejohn.

"You scared the hell outta me! You're way too close. Pull back!"

The tall skinny man peered down at him, a wide grin washing over his face. His bare chest was streaked with big red scratches and streaks of blood.

"Today is a good day to die," answered Littlejohn, as he set down the rifle and picked up an M79 grenade launcher that lay nearby. He pushed the safety forward and pulled the trigger. The weapon made a THUNK sound as the 40mm round left its barrel. A heartbeat later, the earth scattered upward near a pair of tan-clad figures in the distance.

"Listen, you big jerk," said Ricci. He held up the radio's headset in his hand. "I can't get hold of Simon or Baker. The south perimeter got hit pretty hard. I'm pretty sure they're dead. Big Al's gone too. Donny? No idea. There's a column -"

He tried to scream over the metallic clatter of an M60 machine gun in the next trench. Littlejohn pushed a latch, and the M79's barrel fell open. The expended cartridge slid out and tumbled into the hole. Littlejohn pointed his hand out like Babe Ruth just before hitting a homerun. Ricci looked in the direction of the finger.

Another squad of NVA rushed towards them. This time they were organized enough to use covering fire and space themselves out. Littlejohn paid no attention to the dirt kicking up all around his body. He calmly reloaded the Thumper and let off a high explosive round in their direction. The earth shot up near one of the NVA soldiers, who tumbled to the ground and clutched at the growing splotch of bright red on his chest.

Thick bundles of bright tracer fire filled the air around both men. Ricci heard a scream and turned to his right. One of the Hmong fighters nearby groaned while struggling to hold his stomach together.

The wounded Hmong took several deep gasping breaths, closed his eyes, and then reloaded the M60 machine gun. Before he could squeeze the trigger, he slumped down in his hole. The rage that had obscured the Hmong's face dissipated in death.

Ricci recognized the corpse. It was Cho, the boy he had taught English while living among the villagers. Ricci wasn't a great teacher. The boy wasn't a good student. But Cho had learned enough to greet him every morning with a friendly wave of his hand and a beaming smile. "How ya doin'?" he would yell out. Ricci would laugh and call out the same.

And now he was gone forever. Another dead kid. And for what?

Ricci reached up and grabbed the big tall Indian around his throat.

"Hey!" shouted Joe. "Listen! I need to know where these guys are coming from. Where do I direct the air strike?"

Littlejohn looked back at him and waved his hand. "Everywhere, Joe," he said. "The enemy is everywhere."

Ricci's heart fell. Littlejohn was right. They were surrounded. Ban Ngoc couldn't be saved - but maybe it wasn't too late for its inhabitants. He tugged on Littlejohn's sleeve.

"It's time to get outta here."

Littlejohn nodded and stepped up out of the trench as if he were emerging from a swimming pool. Ricci grabbed his friend by the arm and ran towards the center of the village. The clank of oncoming tracked vehicles cut through the commotion.

Ricci tried to shove down the panic welling up inside him. Behind him, the enemy tanks were making slow but inevitable progress over the anti-tank ditches. When they got here, everyone would die. He picked up the handset and set the frequency to match that of the C-130 circling high above.

"Knight Seven to King. Requesting evac at grid coordinates Three One Niner Two Eight Two. I'm gonna need six helos to get these people out of here. Over."

Ricci cradled the set between his shoulder and ear. Each second between the call and response seemed to drag on. Finally, a tinny voice spat out over the static hiss.

"King to Knight Seven. We're sending in one helo for pickup. Over."

Either the controller hadn't heard right or the interference was real bad. Ricci fiddled with the dials and spoke again.

"Uh…negative. Be advised we need approximately six - repeat - six helos for extract. We are under heavy fire and have multiple civilians here who need to be pulled out right now."

While waiting for the reply, a sniper's round sliced through the air above Ricci's head and drilled a nickel-sized hole into the wall. Litteljohn unslung his rifle and fired back while Ricci hunkered down. When the response finally came, he couldn't believe his ears.

"King to Knight Seven, we only have one bird available for evac at this time. That's one bird only. Should be there in five. Pop smoke to show us the pickup zone. Out."

Ricci's mind drifted to the villagers trapped in the middle of the battle. Caught in the crossfire, they were desperate for any way out of here. Then there were the wounded Hmong fighters who would need to be pulled out of here to avoid being captured and tortured by the NVA when they overran the place.

His stomach clenched at the thought of leaving them all behind. Surely, there had to be some way to get them out of this hellhole. He would have to go higher up the chain. Way higher. Ricci knew the CIA area operations officer often accompanied the forward air controllers in the command aircraft to get a bird's eye view of what was happening in his little fiefdom. Perhaps Heath was up there calling the shots. It was time to talk some sense into the man.

"Knight Seven to King. Do you have Windfall with you up there?"

"Wait one."

After a few beats, David Heath's voice poured out over the radio.

"This is Windfall. What's your sitrep?"

Ricci growled out the request again.

"Windfall, this is Knight Seven Actual. Request evac. Six helos. Coordinates as follows."

He pulled out his map again and read off the numbers, enunciating each one clearly. Then he did it again.

When he finally finished, there was a long pause. Ricci listened to the pounding boom of a tank's main gun join with the rattle of heavy machine gun fire. He gritted his teeth and stared at the radio.

"Negative on that request. One Huey inbound on your position. Four minutes."

Ricci shot up as Littlejohn's SVD barked again.

"Dammit!" he said. "How the hell do I get everyone here out on one chopper?!"

Littlejohn ducked his head back around the corner as a hail of gunfire slammed into the nearby wall.

"I'm going back to get whoever else is still alive," said Ricci. "You comin'?"

Both men rushed to the southern perimeter where the first of the T-55s had lumbered across the last anti-tank ditch. The tank's main gun boomed, and one of the two Hmong machine gun nests was obliterated by the blast.

As the turret swiveled towards the other weapons team, one of the Hmong popped up from a foxhole near the tank and fired a handheld anti-tank weapon from less than ten meters away. A stream of smoke marked the path of the rocket from the shooter all the way to his target. The rocket slapped into the vehicle's thick armor, and the turret's rotation stopped.

The Hmong fighters stood up and whooped and cheered. The armored vehicle's coaxial machine gun lit up. Its 7.62mm rounds drummed into their bodies.

Ricci stood frozen in horror as his friends were cut down in front of him. The turret turned his way. While his brain screamed at his body to move, his legs went out from under him as Littlejohn slammed him to the earth. The sand and stones bit into his face.

A hundred meters behind the pair of Americans, one of the village huts blew outward in a hail of earth, wood, and clay. Ricci scrambled out from under Littlejohn's grip. He gestured toward one of the only remaining intact huts in the entire hamlet. A child no older than two years old wandered out the doorway before a hand yanked her back inside.

Ricci pointed. "Che! Let's get Che and her kids the hell out of there!"

Both men sprinted towards the hut, keeping their heads down as the fighting grew more intense all around them. It was down to hand-to-hand combat now. Just within spitting distance, one of the Hmong fighters thrust a bayonet into the belly of an NVA soldier.

Beside him lay a bloodied unmoving figure. The blue jeans and blonde hair could only be that of Don Harris. Ricci's heart fell. Donny the laid-back California kid who would stay up all night and talk about fixing cars - was gone.

Feeling as if the world had dropped out from under his feet, Ricci scrambled up the steps of Che's hut and ran through the open doorway, hoping to find the young mother and her two young children. Instead, he nearly ran straight into a pair of North Vietnamese soldiers. One of them shouted angrily as he turned to see the pair of American intruders. At the back of the hut, the Hmong family huddled together and wailed.

Ricci raised his M16 and squeezed the trigger only to be rewarded with the hollow click. There was no time to clear the jam. He lifted the rifle above his shoulder and threw it like a javelin at the nearest NVA soldier, who deflected it with his rifle. The distraction gave Ricci just enough of an opening to rush towards the man, with his arms spread wide. Just before he made the tackle, he heard Littlejohn rush through the door behind him and fire at the other NVA soldier.

They tumbled to the ground together. The squat enemy grunted as Ricci slammed him down on the hard wooden floor and wrapped his arms around his throat. The tendons in Ricci's arms rippled as he squeezed tighter and tighter. The NVA soldier shouted and threw his hips upwards, sending Ricci sideways to the ground.

In a flash, they both stood up. The NVA soldier reached into his belt and tugged at the scabbard. A knife flashed in his hands. His mouth twisted in sneering contempt. He took one heaving breath and lunged. There was no time for Ricci to get out of the way. Instinctively he threw up his hands and waited for the stab of pain.

A shot bellowed.

The NVA soldier fell lifelessly to the earth. The knife dropped from his grip and clattered on the ground. His eyes met Ricci and he mouthed something before laying his head down as if he were going to sleep.

Littlejohn walked over and said something to Che and the children. His voice was deep, quiet, and commanding. The sobbing subsided, and the children's shrieks turned into soft whimpers.

Ricci breathed in deep. The world was alive all around him with the howl of fighting, and dying, and screaming just outside the hut. A tank fired. He squeezed his eyes shut and waited for the hut to explode around him. When it didn't, he unholstered his pistol and turned to Littlejohn.

"We gotta go," Ricci said to them. "Come on."

The woman scooped up her children with both hands and followed, running behind Ricci and Littlejohn out into the village. Ricci's lungs filled with the acrid smoke from the nearby burning huts. He coughed and sputtered as he sprinted past the foxholes crammed full of Hmong and NVA fighters. Overhead, a lone UH-1 Huey helicopter slapped at the air as enemy tracers hurtled towards it.

"Go! Go!" shouted Ricci. They ducked into the hole in the ground at the edge of the village. Once inside, Ricci led them through the darkness of the makeshift tunnel. The children screamed in terror. Che urged them on, the calm reassurance wading through her words.

By the time they emerged from the other end, the helicopter was already drifting down towards the floor of the jungle clearing. The rotors whipped up the wind all around him as he helped Littlejohn and the young mother and children climb up to the surface.

Ricci stepped on the skids. The crew chief, manning the M60 machine gun screamed. "Come on! Let's go!"

Littlejohn shoved the family toward the waiting Huey. Ricci called out in Hmong to them. "It's okay! Let's go!" He waved and smiled as they edged forward to the helicopter. Thirty meters away, the earth spewed upward near the tree line. Ricci kept the smile riveted on his face though his body screamed in near-panic, knowing the NVA up on the hillside were ranging in their mortars here. Soon, the whole clearing would be wiped out by 60mm shells.

As the children approached, the pilot turned. "We gotta get outta here!"

"Wait!" screamed Ricci. He stepped down from the skids and grabbed the two children by the arms and hoisted them aboard. Littlejohn took the woman by the hands as she neared the Huey. Another mortar round detonated; this time close enough for the fragments to slap into the side of the helicopter. Ricci grabbed the door handle as the Huey leaped upwards. He turned his head and glimpsed the ancient village from the air as they sped away.

Nothing was left. The once-peaceful place where Ricci had lived and laughed and slept among its people was just gone. In its place was a collection of fire and death and human misery. Ricci felt the hot tears on his cheeks as the distance grew between him and the destruction.

So many questions lingered in his head. Why hadn't they all been evacuated? Ricci knew the area of operations well enough. There were plenty of helicopters.

Someone somewhere had merely decided that a group of people was not worth saving - that their lives meant nothing. Heath. When he got back to base, he would have a word with the man and then he would resign. This was it. No more running around in the bush watching his friends die.

As the helicopter flew south, a sinking sensation flooded his conscience. The spot he sat in could have been used for some- one else. In their hour of need, he too had chosen to abandon his friends. He turned away from the sight of the burning village and muttered an apology.

The rest of the way home was spent with Ricci's face buried in his hands.

BLOOD MOON

NATO Condemns Warsaw Pact Invasion
May 2, 1985

BRUSSELS (Reuters) - NATO foreign ministers issued a joint statement yesterday condemning the invasion of West Germany by Warsaw Pact military forces. The press release was issued yesterday evening as a briefing by Pentagon officials showed the Soviet Union and its Eastern European allies had made significant gains in the first twenty-four hours of the war.

At a press conference held at NATO headquarters in Brussels last night, NATO spokesman Jamie Shea read out the strongly worded statement signed by all sixteen member nations. "NATO roundly condemns the unprovoked hostile actions of the Soviet Union and its military allies," said Shea. The release went on to demand an immediate halt to the hostilities and for all Warsaw Pact military forces to return to their pre-May 1 positions. As of press time, there has been no official Soviet response to the NATO statement.

The press event coincided with a live television briefing by General Roger Bernard, a special advisor to the Reagan White House and Joint Chiefs of Staff. Bernard, a 34-year veteran of the US Army, showed a large map that revealed the Warsaw Pact military forces had advanced as far as the Elbe River in some areas.

Several major West German cities including Hamburg, Bremer-haven, and Regensburg have either been captured or have lost communication with NATO forces. Despite the early setbacks, Bernard assured reporters that the Warsaw Pact advances would be "contained" as NATO air power returned to the skies following pre-emptive chemical attacks on military airfields throughout West Germany.

Hostilities have broken out in other regions of the world with reports of clashes along the demilitarized zone between North and South Korea. In Central America, the Nicaraguan President Daniel Ortega has declared his country as a "staunch ally of communism in the open struggle between the forces of freedom and oppression." Reports of FSLN forces crossing the border north into Honduras have been confirmed by anonymous Pentagon officials.

The hostilities began after US President Reagan's televised speech on Tuesday evening warning the Soviet Union to draw down a covert military build-up near the West German border. After revealing photographic evidence of tanks and troops hidden among the forests of East Germany, the president raised the world-wide US military alert level to DEFCON TWO, the highest it had been since the Cuban Missile Crisis.

In a Wednesday morning press briefing, Pentagon spokesman Frank Hoffman confirmed reports that the Soviets and their War-saw Pact allies had sent military forces west over the Inner German Border. In a brief statement released by TASS, the Soviet Politburo declared that the recent years of increasing military aggression by the West could no longer be tolerated and that the operations being undertaken were "defensive in nature"

GHOSTS

Fort Benning, Georgia
May 3, 1985

Ricci threw the folder on the table in disgust.

"Where in the hell did you dig up these guys, Baker? One of them's sixty-five years old!"

Colonel Scott Baker held up a hand. "Look, Joe - I get it. You work with what you've got. Setting up an insurgency over there is… well, not easy."

Ricci chuckled and plucked a faded black-and-white photo from the thick manila folder. The portrait showed a handsome young man standing tall in a tailored uniform, his hair parted and slicked back. A neat row of medals lay across his chest. One of them was quite obviously an Iron Cross.

"Don't give me that! This guy's a Nazi!" said Ricci.

Baker stubbed out the cigarette in the ashtray and ran a hand through his prematurely graying hair. "Wehrmacht," he said. "Not SS. Big difference."

"I don't care," said Ricci. "You're asking me to go over there and start up an operation with these…rejects in hopes of what? Starting up the Fourth Reich? I mean jeez, Baker…did 'Nam scramble your brains that bad?"

It was Baker's turn to laugh. "I think it scrambled all our brains, Joe. We had all kinds of people working for us over there, if you remember. Plenty of shady characters. And hey, if that doesn't help convince you then may I remind you that you owe me one?"

Ricci smiled and leaned back in the office chair, puffing on a Marlboro and resting a hand on the growing paunch that served as the first early sign of encroaching middle age.

"You want me to apologize again to you for leaving you in the jungle?" Ricci said. "Well, sorry. Again. As I said - Ned and I thought you guys were dead. Those tanks came rolling right through your ambush. We hung around for as long as we could." The little voice in the back of his head was full of doubt. Part of him still believed he should have died back there. The guilt and horror he felt during the helicopter ride back to base had never really left him.

"Three days spent humping the boonies on a bad leg," said Baker. "Anyway, it's damn good to see you again after all these years. I know how this thing looks. It's real bad. But once the balloon went up over there, things went crazy. Heath came here and asked me to get someone who had experience leading insurgencies and your name and Ned Littlejohn's name is on this old list. We talked to him and you were next."

Ricci leaned forward at the sound of his friend's name.

"You found Ned?!" he said.

"It's a long story but yeah…we found him. Living in a trailer alone out in the Nevada desert. Still a beanpole who doesn't say but two words when you speak to him. But yeah - we talked."

Ricci laid his cigarette in the tray. "How is he?"

He had sent a half-dozen letters to Littlejohn in the year following their return home from the war, but an answer never came. Eventually, Ricci had just given up. He had assumed his old friend was either dead or, more likely, just wanted to move on with his life and forget the war ever happened. Who could blame him? Baker was the only one who had bothered to keep in touch with an occasional Christmas card or letter. Ricci wondered if the reason for that had something to do with why he had been called here today.

The man had stayed in the army after 'Nam and made a decent career out of it. Fort Benning was a choice assignment. You didn't get here without knowing how to call in favors.

Baker patted the desk with his open palm as if he were playing a card. "Ned is in," he said.

Ricci shot up from his chair. "What?!"

When they had left Vietnam, Littlejohn had been a shell of a man. Near the end, he'd been calling in air strikes on the Ho Chi Minh Trail. One day he came back and looked as if he'd seen a ghost. No matter what Ricci said, the guy just wasn't the same anymore. Ricci had thought he'd finally come around to see the futility of the whole venture. They had gone over there to help people but instead had simply exchanged their youth for a pack of lies. What did Ned think he was going to accomplish by getting involved in another war? Ricci had to find him. Talk some sense into the guy.

"You got Ned's number? It's been a while, and I'd like to get in touch."

"Yeah, I got it. Locked away in a file cabinet. I just need a yes," said Baker.

The man's tone was clear enough. Ricci would never see or hear from Ned again if he walked out the door. He looked at the framed old photo of six smiling young men in olive drab uniforms topped off with green berets. There they were - the ghosts he had lived among for the past fifteen years. There was Big Al, Don, Simon, Baker, Ned, and of course, himself. With their lean frames and unlined faces, they were the very essence of youthful spirit about to embark on an adventure. Their wide eyes and bright smiles beckoned. Something deep inside Ricci ached to say yes, to give in to its filthy allure.

But the mirrored reflection of the unkempt overweight man was enough to convince him otherwise. Joe Ricci was no longer a young man with dreams and hopes. He was a Philadelphia cop with a dead wife and a mortgage and bills to pay. It wasn't pretty but these were the responsibilities of an adult.

Ricci threw his hands up. "No, Chet," he said. "I can't do it. Tell Ned I said hi. Tell him…"

Baker shrugged. "I'll tell him." He stood up and shook Ricci's hand. "I guess you have your work cut out for you up in Philly. Give Veronica my love."

Veronica.

The name struck him like thunder. Ricci almost said it. Almost told him the script he had taught himself to speak as matter-of-factly as possible when strangers mentioned her name in the present tense. It went something like this:

Actually, Ronnie passed away a couple years ago. Cancer. Yeah, came on sudden. Nah, it's alright. She went peacefully in her sleep.

The rest was merely a matter of acting out a play, the purpose of which was to keep everyone at a safe emotional distance. The announcement would be followed by an awkward silence in the room, giving the appearance of shock and grief. Then the words would come in minor variations. "I'm so sorry. If there's anything I can do…"

Instead he faked a smile. "I'll certainly tell her for you," said Ricci.

Baker opened the door for him. Ricci walked down the hallway where men and women in uniforms rushed back and forth with sheaves of papers and printouts in both hands. The sound of boots on polished floor plucked at something inside of him. He tried his best to ignore it.

Once in the car, Ricci drove through the myriad layers of heightened base security and then merged with the wall-to-wall rush hour traffic on I-185, flicking through the local AM radio stations. "…NATO's spokesman has confirmed a large-scale Soviet military force has moved west across the inner German border. Meanwhile, President Reagan, in last night's televised address urged Americans to remain calm and pray for a quick end to the crisis-." Ricci snapped off the radio and drove in silence, finally stopping in front of the run-down motel where he had slept last night.

He thought about taking a short rest before the fifteen-hour drive back to Philadelphia, but quickly dismissed it. He had woken up this morning to find a family of cockroaches skittering across his room's bathtub. The prospect of waking up again to yet more wildlife adventures held little appeal.

He would make a quick stop at the hotel to grab his luggage, return the room key, and settle in for the long drive back home.

Ricci stood outside his room and reached out for the old brass doorknob. Before his hand met the door, his eyes locked on to the fresh scratch that ran through the paint near the lock's mouth. Whoever had tried to pick the lock had done a decent enough job of it. A civilian would probably never have guessed what happened. A ten-year veteran of the North-Central Division assigned to the Robbery unit, however, saw it right away.

He looked around at the vagrants wandering the sidewalk. Inside the room, they would find very little of value in Ricci's luggage - an electric razor, a toothbrush, and a bit of spending money if they looked hard enough. He knew from experience that they had probably seen him coming a mile away and were already gone. But there was always that one lousy day waiting around to surprise you. He shrugged and walked back to the car.

Inside the rusting Chevrolet, Ricci opened the glove box and removed his service weapon. Carrying it low and walking fast, he stopped again at the door and counted silently to three. Just as he reached to turn the knob, it twisted and the door swung open. Ricci took an awkward step back and raised his weapon. "Freeze, scumbag!" he shouted.

There in the doorway stood Ned Littlejohn wearing a faded red checkered shirt and a patched-up pair of blue jeans. A few lines creased the skin under his eyes - otherwise the man had not changed one bit in fifteen long years. Ricci guffawed. A sudden warmth swept through him - as if he had come home after a long time away.

"Ned! Ha! You big beautiful jerk! How the hell are you?"

Littlejohn gave a faint grin and nodded. "Okay, Joe."

"What are you doing in my motel room!?"

Littlejohn shrugged. "Watching TV."

Ricci shook his head and laughed it off. But the questions reeled in his mind. Had Ned been following him around this whole time? Did Baker tell him where he was staying? If so, how did he know?

"Hey, Joe?" said Ned.

"Yeah? What do you need, buddy? You name it. Anything."

"Your gun."

Ricci's face went hot as he realized he had been holding his best friend at gunpoint for the last ten seconds. He tucked the weapon in his waistband and shrugged.

"Yeah, Ned. Sorry about that."

FAMILY PORTRAIT

The motel room was lit only by the soft muted glow of the television screen. Littlejohn had apparently chosen to watch The Smurfs on mute instead of drinking in the unceasing barrage of news about the war that kept every American riveted to the screen these days. Ricci sat at the edge of the single bed, its sheets neatly tucked at the corners, boot camp style. He reached over and plucked the two warm beers that sat on the nightstand, tossing one to Littlejohn and keeping one for himself.

"I know it's early," said Ricci. "But what the hell, right?" The can hissed as he pulled on the tab and held it up in a toast.

Littlejohn turned over the can slowly in his shaking hands. He was silent for a long moment and then handed the can back over to Ricci.

"Better not, Joe," he said.

Ricci grabbed the can and emptied his full beer out in the sink. Usually he felt only pity and disgust for the lowlife junkies that were part and parcel of police work up in Philly. But with Ned, it was different - there was no judgment here.

Everyone dealt with 'Nam differently. Some of them dove into an addiction. Others threw themselves at something in a bid to keep the memories at bay. For Ricci, recovery had meant putting in lots of unpaid overtime on cold cases.

A breakthrough on a forty-year old crime had earned Ricci exactly zero arrests and a permanent position behind a desk in the darkest corner of the precinct. His captain had misunderstood Ricci's initiative as a call for help to get off the streets. The truth was far more disturbing.

Littlejohn sat silent; his gaze fixed straight ahead at the television. Ricci searched for something to say. Surely, there had to be some safe opening.

"I wrote you," he said. "I guess the letters got lost in the mail."

With his eyes still locked on the TV screen, Littlejohn leaned over and dug into his burlap bag and pulled out a thick bundle of papers. Ricci squinted in the darkness. Between Ned's long slender fingers was a stack of letters. The top one was Ricci's earliest attempt at communication, sent nearly fifteen years ago. The folds of the yellowed paper were heavily creased, and several pages were kept together only with the aid of countless pieces of scotch tape. Evidently, Littlejohn had read them more than once. Way more than once.

"I got them," said Ned. "Thanks."

Ricci shook his head. He tried to make the next words come out gently, but he failed to hide his annoyance.

"Why," he demanded, "didn't you write back? I mean, not even once?"

Littlejohn shrugged.

"No money, Joe."

"Are you…are you seriously trying to tell me you couldn't afford a stamp?"

Ricci stood up and fumbled with the knobs on the television until he managed to turn it off. The room turned black. He threw open the curtains on the barred windows. Harsh daylight spilled over Littlejohn's upper body. Ricci paused as he noticed the faint scars running along his friend's forearms. He had seen people with such damage before - but they were almost always in a morgue. His anger evaporated, replaced by the realization that Littlejohn had probably used the darkness to hide a painful truth about his past.

Without even trying, Ricci had made a huge mess of things. What was the right way forward?

He reached for his wallet on the dresser and yanked out all the cash inside then thrust the wad of bills at his friend.

"Take this, Ned," said Ricci. "I owe you, anyway. Remember that poker game in Korat? I cheated. Just take it."

Littlejohn took the money and pocketed it. "Okay."

So that was it, thought Ricci. Littlejohn was desperately broke. That's why he had taken Baker's job offer. Was everything about money? As a cop, Ricci already knew the answer.

Littlejohn got up. Ricci moved to the doorway and stood firm.

"Listen - this whole thing with Baker. I know all about it. It's crazy. You don't need to do it," he said. "Come back north with me. I can help you find a job and a place up there. You can stay with me 'til you get it figured out. Hell, you can stay as long as you want! I got plenty of room. Come on. Whaddya say?"

Littlejohn shook his head and stepped forward. "Gotta go, Joe."

Ricci stood his ground in the doorway. "Why? Why the hell do you want to get involved in another war that has nothing to do with you? Are you some kinda super patriot? Because the last time I checked, this country didn't do your people a whole lotta favors. They practically washed their hands of all us when we got back.

"Did I tell you about when I made it home and I was waiting at Penn Station for the bus? Some hippies spat at me! Called me a baby killer! And you wanna go off and go through all that again? You're nuts, Ned! No amount of money's worth it. Do you…do you remember that time at Ban Ngoc when we had to run off and let everyone die 'cause Heath refused to evac the village? We did nothing over there. It was all a lie. And you're stupid for falling for it again. Don't do it, Ned. Please!"

"See you, Joe," said Littlejohn.

Ricci pounded a fist on the door. "Why?! Tell me!"

Littlejohn shrugged. "I can help."

"Help what, Joe? Help get people killed? Who did we help over there? Huh?"

Littlejohn held up the thick stack of letters. Ricci snatched them and thumbed through the envelopes. Beneath his letters, he found an envelope with an address scrawled in crudely written English.

The stamp on the upper right corner featured a tiny portrait of Thailand's king. Above his head appeared a banner that read "1971". Stuffed inside the envelope was a brief letter written in cursory English. Within the thick white borders of a grainy old photo were the faces of a young mother and her two small children with playful smiles on their faces. It looked a lot like Che and her two kids.

"These are the people we saved at Ban Ngoc?" asked Ricci.

Littlejohn nodded.

Ricci felt a hot tear roll down his cheeks as he brought out the next envelope. The king's image dominated the stamp again, but this time the banner was below the portrait, and the year was marked "1972". Another photo. Two smiling children. On and on it went with each annual envelope bearing an enclosed photograph. The children aged into their teen years and the black and white images gave way to muddy color pictures. The most recent was a photo of three women, two of whom were beautiful young adults. One held a baby in her arms.

Ricci handed back the letters with trembling hands. He walked over to the bed and sat down. The world spun. Until now, his Vietnam experience had been something to forget. Now, it was something else entirely. He had saved a family. Had he merely done what anyone would have, given the same situation? Or had Littlejohn found the one thing that made it all worth it? It was too much to consider.

The motel room door clicked shut. Ricci looked up. Littlejohn was gone.

A hollow emptiness rang out all around the motel room. Ricci was utterly alone now. Another person he cared for had left - the last one, in fact. Soon he would drive back home to Philadelphia by himself. When he got there, he would arrive at his empty home. The next day, he would go to work and sit by himself at a desk. The sheer overwhelming loneliness of it all was enough to make him think about the Model 27 in his waistband. It would be so easy to pull it out and do it. Heck, the nukes would fly any day now - it would probably be a mercy. And who would care? Who would find him here? Perhaps some poor cleaner who would have to mop everything up and then go home to her kids.

Ricci shook his head. If he was going to die for something, he would make sure that something had a meaning. And the only thing that meant anything to him anymore had just walked out the door.

With one giant grunt, he got up and strode out of the motel room.

Littlejohn stood on the edge of the highway, his burlap sack slung over one shoulder, and a thumb extended upwards. Most of the cars and trucks roared by, but one of them slowed down and pulled over to the side of the road.

"Ned!" shouted Ricci. The roar of the busy highway drowned out his calls.

Littlejohn jogged towards the waiting car. When he got near its trunk, a soft drink can shot out of the passenger side window, and landed squarely in the center of his chest. The teenagers inside the vehicle stuck their heads out the window and laughed as the car peeled off.

Ricci ran up to his friend, whose shirt and pants were stained dark with soda.

"Ned! You're a mess!" he laughed. "Look at you! Let's get you cleaned up. Then we'll drive over to the base together. We better get this mission planned or they'll screw us over again."

The corners of Littlejohn's mouth ticked upwards. "You're coming, Joe?"

Ricci picked up the soda can and led his friend back towards the motel.

"Yeah," he shrugged. "What the hell."

CRACKDOWN

Reagan Voices Support for East Bloc Protesters
May 3, 1985

WASHINGTON (AP) - President Ronald Reagan vowed yesterday to assist the "bright forces of democratic resistance" in Eastern European countries following the recent bloody crackdown on Polish anti-war protests.

During the president's weekly radio address to the nation yesterday, Reagan said the demonstrators showed the "spirit and strength of freedom-loving people to resist communist tyranny around the globe." The president's words come on the heels of western intelligence reports and smuggled footage of Soviet tanks firing on protesters in Artur Zawisza Square last Thursday.

Reagan used most of the time in his radio address to strongly condemn the Soviet government's armed response to the nationwide protests. "Their callous disregard of human rights shows that they are a force of evil in the modern world," he told an estimated 70 million listeners on Sunday.

The president went on to say that the US and its allies would pledge their total support for democratic movements in Eastern Bloc countries. "The time for idle talk is long past. We must act now to show our resolve to liberate the human race from oppression in this struggle between right and wrong."

Through the recently invoked Presidential Emergency Powers Act, Reagan said he would find ways to foster and protect such movements. "On Friday, I issued an executive order as commander-in-chief for the allocation of funds and personnel to assist these brave movements," he said.

While the exact details of the provisions were unavailable to the public, an anonymous source in the White House has claimed that more than $5 billion and over 10,000 military advisers will be mobilized.

FIGHTING SOLDIERS FROM THE SKY

Fort Benning, Georgia
May 3, 1985

Shrill warbling tones pried Joe Ricci's eyes open. He found himself alone in a room awash in the soft nuclear glow of the alarm clock's red digits. Slowly he tried to piece together his world as he rubbed his eyes and pulled the blanket over his head.

The infernal angry beeping assaulted his senses, denying every attempt to conjure forth reason. At last, the words fell out of his dry mouth in gravelly protest. "Please," he begged. "Just ten more minutes."

No matter how much he pleaded, the little device refused his every demand. Ricci fell out of bed, his muscles registering the bitter shock of the floor's impact. Each movement was a battle, the completion of which was a hard-fought victory. He grunted and muttered strange syllables as he crawled towards the desk where the alarm clock sat like an angry god punishing him for every trans- gression of a wayward life. Finally, he covered the yawning gulf that separated him from the clock.

With the prize in his hands, his fingers wandered along the surface of the gadget, flicking and pushing its million buttons and switches. At long last, the digital screams turned into the compara- tively pleasant hiss of radio static.

With this monumental task performed, he summoned the willpower to stand up and fumble along the nearest wall for the light switch. The harsh fluorescent light blinked on, revealing the sterile walls and barren lockers of the junior officer's quarters. Ricci nearly laughed. It was precisely how he had remembered the place all those years ago just before he left for Vietnam. It was oddly comforting to know that there were some things that time - nor the military - did not change.

Looking through the rain-speckled window pane, Ricci watched as pallets of cargo laid out on the parade square were loaded on to a long line of 5-ton trucks. Clerks ran between buildings with thick stacks of paper in their hands. Chinook helicopters cut through the low-hanging cloud, rattling the windows and sending little vibrations through the wooden barracks block. Fort Benning was a base at war.

As he squeezed into his moth-eaten olive drab fatigues, Ricci's brain conjured snippets of imagery from yesterday. First, there had been the mountain of paperwork that always went with working for the government. After he and Ned had signed their lives away once again, there were the health checks that poked and prodded at places that Ricci didn't even know he had.

The doctor tsked at Ricci's weight and gasped at the raspy sound of his water-clogged lungs through the stethoscope. Before he left the examination room, Ricci had been told three times that he was in no shape to join any military and warned at least twice to consider some serious lifestyle changes to avoid an early death.

Then it was time to get familiar with the weapons - new and old. They field-stripped, disassembled, reassembled, and fired the Army's latest toys again and again. Not much of it had changed in fifteen years, but it was nice to have a refresher. The biggest surprise was the Stinger air-to-air missile, which he learned how to fire with ease and accuracy thanks to the comic book that served as the launcher's instruction manual.

The kit had changed since Vietnam. It was lighter due to the use of plastic materials. The web gear was also miles ahead of the clunky but functional MCLE load-bearing equipment he had been issued all those years ago.

The newer ALICE gear helped distribute the weight more evenly. Although you were carrying the same load, it felt lighter. Considering that much of the mission would be spent trudging through the bush, that alone was excellent news.

The footwear was still uncomfortable, and the heavy combat boots dug into the soles of Ricci's feet. He winced as he pulled his wool socks over the blisters that dotted his soles. Last came the green beret. Soft, molded, and with the liner removed, it sat comfortably on his head as a silent statement that he had paid his dues in blood, sweat, and tears. He hadn't worn one since he'd come home from 'Nam and once he put it at the back of his closet, he never expected to don it again. Looking in the mirror, he took heart in the fact that even though it was many years ago, he had earned it. The beret was rightfully his. The intervening years and the politics could never take it away from him.

By the time he was dressed, the first murky light of dawn filtered through the blinds. Ricci glanced at his watch and decided it was too early for breakfast. He went over to the radio alarm clock and fiddled with the dials until the static turned into a human voice. Instead of the usual Top 40, the local DJ read the latest news of the war in a somber tone.

"...presented evidence of chemical weapon use in West Berlin. In an emergency UN meeting, East German representative Harry Ott walked out of the meeting chambers as Moscow delegates vehemently denied the accusations. Here in the United States, martial law has been declared in over 200 counties as reports of looting and widespread violent crime have skyrocketed since the initiation of hostilities between NATO and the Warsaw Pact-"

A single knock came at the door. Ricci opened it to find Littlejohn standing there in his fatigues. Just like always, they hung loose over his friend's lean frame.

"Breakfast," he said.

With that, they headed off to the mess hall. When the weary cooks finished slapping the scrambled runny eggs onto their trays, both men tried to find a seat. A few of the younger soldiers stood up as Ricci and Littlejohn wandered around. A fresh-faced lieutenant gestured to the table. "Sir, you can have our seats," he said.

Ricci looked at their trays, filled with uneaten grits and toast. "You're not finished yet," he said.

The kid looked up at Ricci's beret and swallowed. "That's okay, sir. It's all yours." The men stood up and left. Ricci shrugged. He couldn't blame them. With their old Vietnam fatigues on, they must have looked like geriatrics in here. Ricci looked around at the faces in the room, taking the measure of the sideways glances that came their way. At forty-five years old, he was by far the oldest man here.

"I feel like a dinosaur," said Ricci. Littlejohn said nothing as he gazed out the window.

Ricci played with his breakfast and picked up a tattered copy of the morning paper. A glimpse of The Ledger-Enquirer headlines showed a world that had gone insane.

FIERCE FIGHTING IN WEST GERMANY
ATTACKS PUT NATO AIRFIELDS OUT OF ACTION
DPRK ADVANCES SOUTH: SEOUL IN RUINS

Ricci scanned through the worn pages, stopping to read the latest news about Philadelphia. Mayor Goode had finally had enough of the mounting death toll and crime wave spurred on by the war's onset. The National Guard had been called in to restore order in the city.

"Well, that's it then," he muttered softly. "They won't be needing me."

With a curfew declared and the Guard taking over law enforcement duties, Ricci's civilian fate was sealed. His precinct captain would confine him to his desk to type up a mountain of reports. Being back in the army wasn't much better, but at least he had a friend around. He looked up from the newspaper to see Littlejohn, still absorbed in the frantic activity outside. Ricci grinned.

Someone nearby cleared his throat just a little too loud. Colonel Baker stood there in his uniform; the green beret perched on his head.

"Gentlemen, I hate to disturb your breakfast, but we have a lot of work to do today," he said. "In less than twenty-four hours, you'll be in Europe."

Ricci nodded and followed Baker out, Littlejohn in tow. His calves barked at him during the long walk down a busy hallway.

Ricci winced with each step and prayed there would be no more running today.

Baker spun around before they reached the set of double doors, halting the trio's progress.

"Before we go in," said the colonel. "I need to tell you something."

Ricci closed his eyes. "Here it comes!"

"What happened in 'Nam happened. This is a new ballgame and we need to play together as a team. Joe - I know you have grudges. But you gotta let them go. Just for a few minutes more. I need you to hang on."

"I think I know what this is about," said Ricci.

The double doors opened into a large soundproof briefing room covered in gray foam. A scrawny black kid wearing thick square glasses and fatigues shot up to attention as the men entered. Ricci looked the boy up and down, but he wore no insignia or nametag. If he was Special Forces, he certainly didn't look it. He seemed more at home in a junior high school science fair than a war zone.

"Captain Ricci. Sergeant Littlejohn. This is Corporal Lemar Jones. He's a 25U - a signals support specialist direct from the 369th Battalion over at Fort Gordon. He comes highly recommended."

Jones looked visibly uncomfortable from the attention, as if he had been singled out in class for writing an above-average term paper. He stood at attention, swaying in the breeze like a drunkard. Ricci nodded and tried to put the kid at ease with an awkward smile. "As you were, son," he said. Jones collapsed into his chair, the relief sliding over his face.

Baker stood at the head of the table. The door at the other end of the room swung open. Out walked a man from Joe Ricci's past - someone whom he had hoped never to meet again.

"Gentlemen, I believe you know each other," said Baker. "This is David Heath. He's currently the Director of Operations at the CIA."

The room was silent as Heath shook hands with Jones and Littlejohn. Ricci folded his arms when it came to his turn. Both men glared at each other then Heath cleared his throat and spoke in neat practiced paragraphs.

"As you know, we've been engaged in a forty-year conflict between the forces of liberal democracy versus those of Marxist-Leninist persuasion. As of last week, the nature of that conflict shifted from a contest of ideology to a conventional test of arms. The main theater of operations is in Central Europe, and we expect the contest to be decided there."

"Your team will be among one of many that will be deployed behind enemy lines to help bring this war to a quick end. Speed and aggression are the two main principles by which you will operate. You will move decisively and swiftly. The longer this conflict continues, the greater the risk that it will spiral out of our control."

Ricci sat back in his chair. The words were polished, and he suspected this was not the first time Heath had delivered this briefing. He had to wonder how many other teams like his were out there already.

Baker pulled out a map of East and West Germany. Using a red magic marker, he drew a jagged line that ran straight south from Bremerhaven to Kassel and then hooked west towards the Rhine before pulling back east towards the Inner German Border.

"As of 0800 Zulu, this is the official Forward Edge of the Battle Area - the front line," continued Heath. "In reality, it's a big lie. All across West Germany, we're stuck with a great big confused mess. We're not sure where some of our units are. We're tangled up with the enemy, fighting in the dark with each other. Battles are small-scale, localized, and very quickly decided. Some of our units have managed to ambush each other out in the chaos."

"Right now, the Russians have made very deep advances into West Germany, especially in the south in the Fulda Gap. They caught us off-guard with the initial attacks and we fell back quickly. The cavalry's been screening the attack but they can't be everywhere. The Soviets are going for the minor bridges, which has thrown us off our game. A recent counterattack near Fulda failed badly when their reinforcements showed up before ours could. It's…a big mess out there for us."

Ricci stared at Heath. The mask was off. His voice trembled just enough for Ricci to know that this was the real deal. There was no mistaking the desperation underneath the formality of the briefing.

"Gentlemen, it has been decided that the enemy will not be beaten only by conventional military means. To win this war, we will have to do so on the micro-level. Small unit actions will make the difference between victory and defeat. To that end, we are sending units like yours to operate independently on the enemy's soil right in the heart of East Germany."

Ricci raised a hand. "Lemme guess. You want us to hit the Soviet reinforcements as they come down the road?"

"That's part of it," said Heath. "But mostly we want you to harass and, if possible, eliminate the Russian garrison in your primary area of operations. If you can imagine a fifty kilometer diameter clock centered around the town of Schönewalde , you'll have a basic understanding for how this operation will work.

"Your team is responsible for everything from the 11 to 1 o'clock slice up to fifty-kilometers out from the center of Schönewalde . The other A-Teams will be operating in the other slices but the less you know about that, the better. The handouts go into further detail on your boundaries and goals. If everyone does their part, we can evict the Russians from the Saxony region."

Baker cleared his throat. "Uh, sir. They don't call it that anymore."

Heath caught himself and chuckled. "Sorry, that's what they called it before the war. The Soviets changed the name of the place and played around with the boundaries. Let's see…what do they call it now – oh yeah, here it is – Bezirk Magdeburg. Just rolls off the tongue, doesn't it?"

Ricci's hand went up. "Why there?"

Baker spoke up. "Schönewalde? It's the headquarters of the 2nd Guards Tank Army. The town itself is pretty much flattened but the military traffic is still moving west through there to feed the attacks against the Brits near Hannover. There are a ton of roads and it serves as a rail hub. The area around it is pretty flat in lots of places but there's plenty of forest cover for you to operate from in your area. If you make good use of the terrain, you'll find what you need."

Heath continued from where he left off.

"Anyway. once we take out enough Russian presence from the area, we can talk to the East German government about withdrawing its support for the war. We've been in secret negotiations with liberal elements of East Bloc governments from the first day."

Ricci thought of the photos Baker had shown him the other day. "And we use your ready-made insurgent teams to accomplish this mission?"

Heath nodded. "You'll be working together with East German insurgents. You'll be supplying, advising, and training them. Liberal elements of the East German government covertly requested this assistance and they've done a little behind the scenes work to give you a bit of breathing room. In exchange for that, the deal is you'll hit Russian targets only."

Ricci smirked. "Would you like to enlighten these other gentlemen about the wonderful people we'll be working with?"

Heath waved a hand. "All thirty of them have…uh…military backgrounds. They were put together quietly by a CIA operation long before the war started. They are anonymous. They don't even know each other's names. Some of them don't speak English, but that shouldn't be a problem for Corporal Jones. He grew up in West Germany. He's fluent in German and Russian. He's also one of the best radio operators in the Western hemisphere. I recommend you employ his fullest capabilities."

"Got it," said Ricci. "We run the playbook just like back in Laos. Find them, hit them, and keep moving. We'll run so deep they won't even know we're there until it's too late."

"About that…," said Baker. "We want to mobilize the civilian population to oppose their country's participation in the war. You'll also have one of the insurgents videotape everything."

Ricci let his hand thump the table. "Videotape? You're not seriously proposing we advertise ourselves."

Heath's eyes narrowed. "Part of the mission is PSYOPS. Don't worry. The tapes will be collected every day during the supply drop and then sent for editing. We have industry professionals working on it. Once the contents have been neatly packaged for an East German audience, they'll be broadcast by an EC-130 flying high above East German airspace."

Ricci threw his head back and laughed. Heath glared.

"You have a comment, Captain Ricci?"

"You're gonna make us famous? With our location and faces sent out over East German TV every day, they'll catch us before the week is up. This whole thing is nuts. Who signed off on this? Reagan?"

Heath nodded. "I was skeptical at first too. But with today's Hollywood special effects and computers, you can do plenty. We're currently broadcasting similar hour-long shows to the East Germans as we speak."

"How long until the Russians come down on us like a hammer?" asked Ricci. "You're asking us to stir up trouble right in their backyard. They'll smoke us out. Or they'll clamp down so tight that we won't be able to move. You saw it yourself in Laos. The NVA came in and destroyed us."

"You've already seen the terrain in the photos," said Heath. "Plenty of forests and hills in the area to hide yourselves. You're resourceful - that's why we picked you. If things get too hot, we can pull you out of there. We're just a helicopter ride away."

"I've heard that before, old friend." Ricci could no longer hide the bitterness behind the words. He hurled them out without a care.

Heath stepped forward. "If you're unhappy with the assignment, Mr. Ricci, it's your privilege to refuse. Say the word and I'll call the MPs and have them escort you off the base."

Baker stepped between the two men and offered up a single sheet of paper.

"Here's what you're up against," he said. "Most of the East German military is sitting in West Germany fighting alongside their Russian comrades. The Soviets have mobilized their Category C divisions to come west and babysit the East Bloc nations. From what we can gather, they're there to keep a lid on things while the rest of the Warsaw Pact is busy fighting us. We don't have much intel on them except that these are rear units - not much in the way of decent training or equipment."

Ricci nodded. It was the first bit of good news he had heard all morning.

Baker continued. "You should set up a listening post early on to find where the major units in the area are located. I believe Corporal Jones will assist you with that. He's been given some very advanced equipment and some special training on radio jamming, interception, and deception."

Ricci had heard of deception operations used in Vietnam. The VC were skilled at the practice and got so good at it that they were able to call in American artillery strikes on US Army units in the field. If this kid could pull that off, he was the most valuable member of the team.

"I'll need a few weeks to get these guys trained and up to speed on the equipment and tactics," said Ricci. "By then we should have a pretty clear picture of what's happening around us."

Heath stepped in.

"Uh…negative. We don't have weeks," he said. "This war's going at an extreme pace. We need you in there and operating within the next three days."

Ricci balked. "Three days! Are you out of your mind?! Even three weeks is barely enough time to get the basics down - you know that! These guys are gonna get slaughtered without any proper training!"

"Look at the profiles," said Baker. "All the insurgents have military training. It's a modern country with mandatory conscription. You're not leading mountain tribesmen who've never seen a gun before."

"Military training. Yeah…the last time some of these guys had military training, they were learning how to goose-step through Poland."

"Captain Ricci, this is not a time where we can afford to be choosy about our allies," said Heath. "If you feel you cannot perform this mission, say so now and I will find your replacement. I have little time to further debate the issue with you." The answer came out in dark tones. Any sane man would have walked away by now. If it weren't for Ned sitting beside him at the table, Ricci would have been long gone, driving north and looking for a Burger King drive-thru on the way to Philly.

Instead, he swallowed his pride and spoke in meek tones that made him hate himself.

"No sir," he said. "We'll work with what we've got."

"Look, it's not as bad as you think," said Heath. "These men were identified and handpicked by us over the course of many years. When the war began, this cell was activated. None of them know each other's name or identity. But they've had a chance to train with each other for four days already. Their leader, Major Werner Brandt, was one of the rising stars in the Volksarmee. His death was faked on the opening day of the war to avoid any repercussions on his family. I'll agree it's a ragtag bunch. But it's better than what we had to deal with in previous conflicts."

Ricci couldn't help but notice the man's aversion to directly referencing Vietnam. He wanted to stand up and scream it in his face. Instead of grappling with the painful scars of the conflict, the country had been in a hurry to forget about it. The result had been a lost decade that cast a cynical shadow over the proud ideals of his country and its politics.

"Are we coordinating with the other insurgent groups in the area?" asked Ricci. "What kind of support do we get from the B-Team?"

Baker nodded. "You are not to move outside your designated area of operations. You run your own missions as you see fit with as little interference as possible."

Ricci liked to hear that. The last thing he needed was another SF team out there breathing down his neck and telling him what to do. On the other hand, it left his group without anyone to call on for assistance. It was like walking a tightrope in a hurricane without a net. The odds of coming home seemed longer the more these men talked.

The rest of the briefing dealt with the details of supplies, weapons, and logistics. Ricci listened carefully and took notes. When it was over, Baker and Heath strode out of the room, leaving the three men alone. Ricci thought he should say something inspiring, but nothing came. There was no sense trying to sugar-coat the crap sandwich that had just been served up.

A dark cloud covered his brain as he realized the enormity of his situation. If the war's course depended on people like him to go out and perform these kinds of missions, they were all in massive trouble indeed. He looked at his watch and stood up.

"Plane leaves in two hours," he announced. "Don't be late."

The helicopter swayed and lurched as it skimmed over the dense forests below. Ricci liked the UH-60 but wished he could ride it like a Huey with his legs sticking out the doors, and his feet on the skids ready to jump off into a hot LZ. He couldn't complain though. It felt good going into action again. Sprawled out fast asleep on the bench beside him was Littlejohn. Siting opposite was Corporal Jones, retching into a paper bag and clinging to the edge of his seat for dear life.

Less than four hours ago, they had arrived in Amsterdam on a C-130 aircraft that was cramped, loud, and uncomfortable. Instead of dozing like the others, Ricci had spent the duration of the flight jawing with a half-dozen Rangers along for the ride. The young men - most of whom were half his age - asked Ricci all kinds of questions about his time spent in Vietnam and Laos.

They listened carefully to his answers, treating him with the respect and reverence reserved for a grandfather. Nice kids, no doubt. But the encounter had left Ricci feeling like he should be scheduling a hip replacement instead of going off to war. He was more than a little relieved when they parted company on the tarmac.

Now it was just the three of them. Ricci noted the familiar sights of war outside the Blackhawk's windows. Towering columns of inky smoke drifted upwards, blotting out the blue sky. Jets blasted through the air high overhead.

More than once, huge glowing tracers from the ground shot upwards, a few meters from where Ricci sat. Instead of the terror he expected, his brain latched on to the excitement. Like a junkie, he was once again hooked on the old adrenaline rush.

The terrain below turned from soft green expanses to rocky and rugged slopes. The helicopter kept low to the ground, swerving around the base of each hill. Ricci's gut registered the rough progress. As he gripped the bench tighter, he admired the Blackhawk's design and agility. It seemed that someone had listened to at least some of the grunts' complaints from Vietnam.

The new helo was roomier, better protected, and more comfortable than the choppers he had ridden in fifteen years ago. Still, he missed the iconic slapping sound of the Huey's rotors. There was something oddly comforting about hearing that racket after a long stint in the bush.

A tap on his shoulder brought his attention to the crew chief. The young man bent over him, a stick of gum held out in his hand. Ricci smiled and took it, nodding thanks.

"'Nam?" he shouted, pointing at Ricci's olive-drab fatigues.

Ricci shrugged. "Yeah."

It wasn't the first time he felt the sting of regret for deciding to wear his old jungle fatigues. They screamed for attention. Ricci couldn't help but wonder at how everyone had suddenly become enamored with Vietnam veterans. Where was all this positive attention fifteen years ago?

"Like your boots?" the chief asked.

Ricci looked down at the shiny new combat boots on his feet. The footwear was the right type for where he was going, but his feet still felt hot and itchy. There was no air circulation down there. They were also heavy. Every step was a battle to spare his calves and heels from the confines of this leather hell. How he wished he hadn't thrown out his old boots after getting back home.

"Not really," he shouted back.

"Size?"

Ricci's eyes narrowed. "Uh…ten."

The chief picked through one of the nearby cardboard boxes stacked on the floor of the helicopter.

Like pulling a rabbit out of a hat, the chief produced a brand new pair of M-1966 jungle combat boots and tossed them at Ricci's feet. He picked them up and admired the vent holes and the canvas upper. They were perfect - just like the ones he had worn back in Laos. Ricci laughed and gave the chief a big thumbs up.

He eyed the rest of the containers stacked inside of the helicopter. Some of them were metal canisters marked as ammunition boxes. The long wooden crates were unmarked, but this was not Ricci's first rodeo. The Defense Department used the same packaging for the rifles and light machine guns used to supply the Hmong. The other boxes were cardboard. Their insides were crammed full of fatigues, MREs, and medical supplies.

"All this is for the Germans?" shouted Ricci.

The chief nodded and gestured to the bounty of goods. "Surplus," he said.

Ricci chuckled and shook his head. It may have been surplus, but there was more stuff in this one shipment than would have gone to the Hmong in an entire month. Clearly, he had moved up to a better class of insurgency. As he rifled through one of the boxes, his headset crackled to life. The pilot's smooth voice slid into his ears over the intercom system. "Two minutes."

Ricci's gut clenched as he put on his heavy pack. He thought about waking Littlejohn then decided against it. He had once nearly paid for doing so with his life. Pinned to the ground with a knife held to his throat, Ricci had begged his friend to wake up before he killed someone. Littlejohn later claimed to have no memory of any of it. The man's reaction was pure instinct.

Two minutes later, the helicopter flared, and its forward momentum slowed as the rear rotor dipped towards the ground. The stack of metal boxes near Ricci teetered. He put out a hand to steady them as the chief swore and leaned against three crates full of claymores.

Finally, the Blackhawk tilted forward again and settled into a hover. Ricci regained his balance just in time to brace himself for the rapid earthward descent. Seconds later, the crew chief slid the van-like doors open. The sights and sounds of the outside world swept in fast, hard, and loud.

The East Germans rushed forward in pairs from the tree line towards the Blackhawk. When they arrived, they grabbed the edges of each crate and rushed off as the next pair came forward and did the same. The crew chief placed a boot on several of the boxes near the door and kicked them out. They tumbled and landed in the tall grass.

When the cargo was gone, Ricci jumped out. His knees tingled with pain as he landed in the clearing. Behind him, Littlejohn simply took one long stride to reach the ground. Jones stood at the doorway of the hovering helicopter, fear branding his face. The crew chief patted his shoulders and gestured for him to jump. The kid's eyes went wide as he realized the pilot had no intention of landing here. Jones half-fell and half-jumped, tumbling awkwardly to the ground.

A young man in dark green fatigues rushed forward, his hand on his angular helmet. The dust from the rotor wash swirled as the Blackhawk lifted up. The man grabbed Ricci by the arm and led him towards the trees. Before he reached the first row of pines, the helicopter was gone. The sound of its rotors receded in the distance. The fun was over. Ricci tried to focus on the mission ahead.

A half-minute later, he was deep inside the forest. The faint rays of sunlight spiked through the canopy of tall trees. They veered off a worn path, stepped over a lazy flowing stream and arrived in the center of another clearing.

"Wait here," said the East German. His accent was thick and surly. He walked off into the trees, leaving Ricci alone in his confusion. The East Germans knew full well they were coming. The signals specialists back at base had sent an encrypted burst transmission less than three hours ago. Somewhere behind him came the little "click" - the sound of a safety being flicked off. Ricci took a deep breath and stood still, curiosity overpowering the urge to panic and run.

"Put down the weapon," a deep voice commanded.

Ricci turned. "I'm friendly. I'm here -"

"Don't turn around! Put your weapon on the ground."

"You just saw me step off a US Army helicopter," Ricci said. "What's your problem?"

"Last chance. Put down the weapon."

"Fine," he muttered. Ricci set his M16A1 on the flat surface of the large rock near his feet. Had they been compromised? Maybe the Russians had been on to them from the start. Ricci tried to stave off the images of what they would do to him. His arm brushed against the butt of the service revolver he had tucked in his waistband. A bead of sweat wound its way down his jawline as the resolve welled up within him.

"Your web gear," said the voice. "Take it off."

Ricci did as he was told, using the quick release to remove the gear and the pack on his back. The bag let out a heavy thud as its contents met the ground.

"Turn around now. Slowly!"

Ricci raised his hands and pivoted. Maybe they would shoot him right here. That wouldn't be so bad. He had almost done it himself two days ago. He closed his eyes and waited for the burst of fire to hit him. Nothing happened.

"Look, I know Brandt's around here somewhere," he said. "Can you go get him for me? I'm sure he can clear-"

From behind one of the trees, a lone figure stepped out. In his hands, he held an assault rifle. The look on his face was of sheer menace. There he was in the flesh. That broad face topped with salt-and-pepper hair. It was Brandt. He looked just like in the photo.

"Major Brandt!" shouted Ricci, laughing. "I nearly crapped myself!" He stepped forward.

Brandt shouldered the AKM, his eyes narrowed. "Don't move," he muttered.

Ricci halted and threw his hands up, his mind spinning. Judging from the death stare on Brandt's face, something had been gone wrong - and now it needed to be repaired very quickly.

"Major Brandt, I'm Joe Ricci," he said. "They told you over the radio I was coming. Remember?" His mind raced as he tried to get at the heart of the problem. Getting shot by an enemy was all part of the game. But friendly fire just sucked.

The leaves rustled and a twig snapped just behind where he stood. Ricci almost turned but forbade his body from making any sudden movements.

A pair of hands patted at his fatigues, stopping only to pull out the sidearm in his belt. When at last the humiliating pat-down was complete, Ricci gritted his teeth.

Brandt shouted. "He's clean?"

A single word was spoken in a deep flat tone. "Clean."

"Alright Ricci," said Brandt, finally lowering his rifle. "Let's get to base camp. Your other men will be along soon."

Ricci bit his lip. He wanted to ask if he'd be strip searched too but this was not the time. Before he shot his mouth off, he needed a better measure of these men. The photos and records of service only told so much of the story.

As he marched through the bush with a rifle aimed in his direction, the indignity of his situation sunk in. Ricci had not even begun the mission yet! The same thought crossed his mind over and over. This was supposed to be the easy part.

After he arrived at yet another clearing in the forest, he was led to a small rustic wooden shed that sat next to a huge dilapidated barn.

Brandt opened the creaking shed door and gestured Ricci inside. The tattered calendar on the wall read "1975". Next to it was a bunk with blankets strewn across the filthy mattress. A scratched wooden desk sat nearby with a Makarov pistol and a framed black and white photo of a happy family. There was a mother in her apron, a father in factory worker's garments, and a small boy whose eyes resembled those of Brandt's. It was "Leave it to Beaver" - the East German edition.

Ricci sat down and pointed to the picture. "Those your parents?"

Brandt nodded. "My mother was beautiful," he murmured.

"Your father was a handsome devil," said Ricci. "Bet he still charms the ladies."

Brandt looked up. "My father is dead. Murdered. June 17th, 1953. I still remember it. There were strikes everywhere. It was electric. On that morning, he went marching with the other workers down the street near our home. I watched the Russians shoot him like a dog. He wasn't doing anything wrong. Just…marching with the others."

The silence dragged on. Ricci squirmed in his seat, unsure of what to say. He was still heated about the way he'd been welcomed. If Brandt was some kind of Colonel Kurtz, then Ricci would have to find a replacement quick. He was not about to deal with a total lunatic to get the job done here. It was time to draw some boundaries and take measure of the man.

"I'm sorry to hear that," said Ricci. "But the way you greeted our arrival was completely unnecessary. I'm not here to run your men for you. I'm an adviser. You're the leader. If there's something you don't want to do, then I won't insist. If you want us to leave, we'll be packed up and gone in twelve hours."

"And if I ask for something, you will find a way to give it to me?" asked Brandt. He leaned forward in his chair and studied Ricci's face.

"That's my call," said Ricci. "If I think the request is reasonable, I'll try my best."

Brandt sneered at the answer. "Well, Mr. Ricci. We all want to help you spread your American brand of freedom and democracy. I'm sure we can work together. Our exploits will be legendary. Like one of your Hollywood movies."

Ricci nearly laughed. "Sir, the stuff that we do here doesn't end up in movies. If all goes well, it barely gets noticed at all. Occasionally, it might register a single line in a newspaper article. Then it's over and forgotten. No history textbooks. No parades."

Brandt cast his eyes away. Ricci made a mental note of it. So the major had an ego. That wasn't necessarily a bad thing. Some of the best leaders in history saw themselves as a figure of glory, unable to do any wrong. What mattered was how much his men would buy into the schtick.

"You've been with your men for a few days now out here," he said. "How do you feel about them?"

Brandt lit a cigarette and took a long drag before exhaling slowly.

"It's a strange mix. Criminals, fools, idealists, liberals, fascists…," Brandt said. "We don't discriminate here. Everyone has their reasons. No one asks too many questions. Everyone wants to kill as many Russians as they can."

"Sounds complicated," said Ricci.

"It will take some time for everyone to adjust, but so far there have been no major issues."

So Brandt wasn't completely blind to his own vulnerabilities. Good. The last thing he needed was a civil war breaking out among these men. They would deal with the bad apples later if they became a problem. Right now, Ricci needed to know what material assets he had to work with.

"You have tanks or vehicles? How are you getting around?" he asked.

The East German major opened a fist to reveal an empty palm. "There are no roads into this part of the forest. The woods are too thick and the ground uneven. Even if we had trucks, the security checkpoints have made road travel more trouble than its worth. For now, we move on foot. It's worked well enough so far."

Brandt pointed out the map on the desk. To the north of Schönewalde, there were several red circles.

"We've been keeping ourselves busy while we were waiting for you," he said. "We liberated a BMP for one of your infiltration teams."

Ricci nodded. "Impressive. I think I read about that in the brief."

"We've also been scouting. These are areas where we have spotted enemy patrols," said Brandt.

"Okay, we'll look at that soon. First, I have to go smash a video camera."

THE AMBUSH

Checken Nature Park Nuthe
15 kilometers north of Schönewalde

Ned Littlejohn pushed away the branch of the pine tree to see who was about to die. Less than a dozen meters from where he crouched, a red-faced middle-aged man wearing an ill-fitting forage cap and sweat-stained tunic trudged along the worn forest path.

Instead of holding his weapon, the man's bolt-action rifle was slung over his shoulder. Gulping at the air, he paused in the clearing and wrested a pack of rolled tobacco from his pocket. When he had finally managed to light the bent cigarette, he took a long drag and used his free hand to wipe the sweat that rolled down his jowls and soaked the edges of his collar.

Behind the heavyset man, two more soldiers ambled along the path and dropped their packs and rifles in the undergrowth. One of them wore a plaid shirt and a pair of faded slacks instead of the Red Army's usual green army fatigues. The other sported frayed combat webbing and a rusting pot-shaped helmet that looked like it predated at least one world war.

The next three members of the patrol came into sight.

One of them staggered through the brush, clinging to the trunks of nearby trees to maintain his balance. Soon, they were all standing in a circle facing one another, chatting and smoking as if they were on a coffee break. The small group of pot-bellied Russians with their gray hair and thick glasses looked more like they belonged in a cozy neighborhood bar than in the middle of a war.

Littlejohn tensed as three more figures crept down the trail. These men were different. In their hands were AKM assault rifles. Instead of civilian clothes, they sported birch-colored Afghanka BDUs of Soviet front-line troops. The dark green stars sewn on their shoulders revealed their rank as officers. Upon their arrival, the smoking circle dispersed like a flock of sparrows disturbed by the presence of a hunter. One of the officers kicked at the old men, who grumbled as they stubbed out cigarettes and formed up into a ragged formation.

A lone member of the group stood quietly and turned his head slowly to look in Littlejohn's direction. Littlejohn tightened his grip on the M16A1 rifle. As he crouched in the thick undergrowth, he held his breath and waited. The Russian officer peered at him with dark eyes set in a weathered face. Littlejohn instantly understood he was looking at the only warrior of the bunch.

The enemy soldier took a slow measured step forward.

Littlejohn flicked off the safety of his rifle.

CLICK.

It seemed as loud as a cannon. He was sure they had heard it. How could they not?

Littlejohn brought the rifle up to his shoulder as the soldier advanced. With the Russian's chest dead center between his sights, he slowly emptied his lungs and settled his finger on the trigger. The initial alarm gave way to a deadly calm focus.

EMBRRRRRT!

The throaty rattle of a hooded crow shot out from high above. The black and white bird suddenly leaped upwards through the branches, then made a lazy wide circle above the Russians. The Russian trained his rifle on it, following the bird's flight before lowering the weapon with a chuckle. He said something to one of the other officers, who laughed and pointed towards where Littlejohn sat. The group of men departed the clearing in a single file.

Through his nostrils, Littlejohn slowly inhaled the pine-scented air into his burning lungs. His grip on the rifle loosened as he lay his finger flat across the trigger guard.

When the group of enemy soldiers was out of sight, Littlejohn keyed his radio twice. Brandt would hear it and get his men ready. He turned around and disappeared back into the forest, knowing that he had just condemned nine men to their deaths. Littlejohn searched for the peace of the sacred warrior within, but it was nowhere to be found. There was only the cold tingling of the last fifteen years. Forgiveness seemed further away than ever. The act of coming here seemed a vain mistake. The vision of an old woman, her face filled with rage, flashed for a moment then disappeared.

As he stalked through the trees, Littlejohn winced as his brain registered a stinging pain in his right index finger. He looked down to see the wasp burrowing its stinger into the flesh. Though his body screamed at him to swat the insect away, he gritted his teeth and allowed the outrage to run its course. Finally, the wasp drifted away, leaving behind a bright dot of blood on Littlejohn's red skin.

***

Werner Brandt held the radio in one trembling hand, the claymore detonator in the other. His stomach was clenched tight, as though it were caught in a vice. He took deep breaths, trying his best to keep the terror at bay. Something awful was about to happen. He checked everything again for the thousandth time.

Security teams were laid out to his right, left, and rear. The assault team was nearby. The claymores were - not again!

Brandt turned over the remote detonator in his sweaty palm, checking once again that he had correctly plugged the blasting wire into the top of the M57 electrical firing device. Three times, he had practiced using the detonator in the ambush rehearsal.

Each time, the claymores had failed to fire.

The two American advisers had to come and troubleshoot for him and verify that it worked. It always went the same. They would test it out and find nothing wrong. But whenever Brandt tried it, he would pound the clacker and nothing would happen. He glared at the stubborn device. The only explanation for the malfunction was that the machine hated him. It didn't make sense at all but it was the only reason left. Now it would have the last laugh as its failure saw to his certain death.

Brandt saw the events in his mind unfold. The Russian patrol would come into the kill zone. He would pound three times on the clacker. Nothing would happen. His men would not know to open fire. The enemy would see the ambush and kill them all. He closed his eyes and pushed back against the fear.

The plan. Focus on the plan.

Brandt mentally reviewed what was about to happen. When the radio signaled the patrol's approach, he and his men would wait for the Russians to enter the kill zone of the L-shaped ambush. The claymores would blow. His machine gunners and riflemen would open fire. When the dust cleared, the assault team would search the enemy dead then cross the road. They had rehearsed it all so many times. The training had made it all seem so simple but reality had a way of complicating matters.

Brandt picked up a clump of dirt and let the soil slip through his fingers. It was all just a matter of gaining experience. He and his men had yet to fire a single shot in anger since the start of the war. This ambush - if it ever happened - would be his and their first taste of real combat. The claymores were just a small part of it.

Like a seafaring captain, he tried to ride the rough tide of endless problems that threatened to capsize his command. Despite the outward appearance of quiet camaraderie among the men, the truth was that cracks were beginning to show. Every day for the last four days, fistfights had broken out, peppered with the occasional brawl.

One of his men had run off last night. Brandt had tried to cover it up. He lied to Ricci and told him that the deserter was merely sick and unable to fall in this morning. Appearances needed to be maintained to keep the Americans satisfied and the steady flow of supplies coming.

If Ricci found out about the problems and shut things down, Brandt would have to arrange for an accident to happen. But that was the least of his worries now.

He glared at the radio again, trying to command it with sheer willpower. All he needed now was just two little clicks. Was it so much to ask? The handset sat stubbornly silent.

He checked over the frequencies and then looked over at "Two", his second-in-command. The man lay there to his left, the American rifle in his hands. Like all the other men, he was camouflaged and concealed in the undergrowth.

Brandt tried to take a swig of his canteen only to find it empty. Shaking his head, he set it down beside him and stifled the urge to shout in frustration. Everything was falling apart. He was hot. The American scout was dead. The radio was not working. The claymores will not go off.

As if in answer to his prayers, two faint clicks came over the handset. His heart soared.

Brandt's arm shot up, making a fist with the thumb pointed down. The machine gun team was to give the same hand signal, serving as an acknowledgment that they had received the "ready" message. The signal would then be passed along to the other men down the line. But nothing happened. He glared at the rough outline of the two prone men less than ten meters away. Both of them were obscured by careful placement of the leaves and foliage from the surrounding forest. He raised his arm again. No response. Were they asleep?

Finally, the leaves stirred. From the heap of vegetation, an arm poked upward. The hand attached to it configured in the same signal. Immediately, a chain reaction of hands shot up all down the line. Brandt nodded and craned his head to the left. "Two" looked back at him and nodded. Everyone was ready.

Brandt tried not to fidget as he waited for the targets to appear. The Russians would all die. Oh, how they would pay for all the hardships they had inflicted on his country! They would pay for Brandt's lost youth and the poverty he and his mother endured. Their children too would come to know what it was like to grow up without a father. He would kill every last one of them.

They would all suffer and beg and plead for mercy, and he would never ever relent.

Slow inhalations through the nose. Long exhalations through the mouth. Thirty years, Brandt had waited for such a moment to come, and now it was so close. For the Russians, there would be chaos, shouting, and terror. But for him, there would only be unfiltered hate.

The minutes passed. Brandt rechecked the clacker. A soft whistling drifted through the trees like a summer day. The happy little tune grew louder as each moment passed. Finally, the dark outline of a man became visible through the leaves and branches. He strained his neck to see the Russian invader stroll down the trail, his eyes trained on the blue skies above. He was fat and old. Brandt felt the bile rise in his throat.

The Russian stepped in the center of the kill box with the rest of the patrol bumbling along behind. Brandt counted the parade of nine future victims, three of whom were armed with automatic weapons and wearing proper uniforms. The first man passed deep into the kill zone. If he had looked hard enough, the idiot would have spotted the claymore mines that lined his route. If he had been cautious, he might have even seen the men laying in the undergrowth only a dozen meters away. Instead, he kept walking straight into the trap like the rest of them. He gave no sign that he understood the danger that was all around them.

Brandt sneered as he watched them. When the man at the rear was even with the first of his machine gun teams, Brandt picked up the clacker, removed the safety, and pulled the trigger three times.

CLACK CLACK CLACK.

Nothing.

CLACK CLACK-BOOM!

The string of claymores detonated with a series of loud sharp bangs. Someone screamed just before the machine guns ripped the Russians apart.

Brandt brought his rifle up and scanned for a target. Seeing nothing but the smoke and dust floating up near the tree line, he switched to automatic and fired several short bursts in the general direction of the enemy. There was a quick blur of motion on the trail. Brandt squeezed the trigger again. After loosing another short burst, he tried to make sense of what was happening. Finally, he gave up and just emptied the magazine into the general direction of where he thought the Russians might be. The fire died off until Brandt reloaded and fired again.

The magazine was dry in seconds. He crawled forward a little out of his foxhole, hoping to catch sight of the enemy. The woods echoed with the sound of automatic weapons fire. Branches and tree limbs exploded and the leaves and twigs rained down on his helmet. He raised his head up high enough to glimpse a pair of legs on the trail. The slacks covering them were shredded and bloodied.

He inched forward toward a leafy shrub, behind which he could gain a better view of the kill zone. Upon the road were heaps of bodies, sprawled in the dirt with their limbs out at awkward angles. Several of the corpses jolted as the machine gun rounds drilled into them. Everyone was dead multiple times over. The sight of it sent an electric shock through Brandt's nervous system. The fiery rage inside of him was not quenched, as he had originally feared. Instead, he quietly mourned that there were not more Russians to kill. For now, though, their bloody work appeared to be finished.

Brandt put up a hand. "Cease fire! Cease fire!" The cacophony of rifle fire continued unabated.

The East German major stood up slowly and ran over to the machine gun. The two-man team lay prone, a pile of brass accumulating beside them. Brandt aimed a kick at the loader's shoulder. The man's head swiveled up to meet Brandt's eyes.

"Cease fire!" shouted Brandt.

The young man nudged the gunner. The firing died down over the next minute and a half until the woods were suddenly silent. Brandt whistled twice. The three-man special team ran from their nearby firing positions towards the trail.

Brandt sighed as one of his men reached the other side without pausing.

The other two soldiers had the presence of mind to stop and pry the weapons from the dead. One of the enemy soldiers on the ground stirred, bending his knee. Brandt emerged from the undergrowth and walked onto the trail. The old Russian looked up at him, his hands shaking as he held up a pack of cigarettes. "Before I die," he pleaded. "Just one."

Brandt swatted the pack away and emptied two shots into the man's skull. He then tossed the enemy weapons far out of reach of the dead men then whistled again. The three-man search team went through the dead Russian soldiers' pockets and backpacks, pulling out papers, diaries, and anything else of potential intelligence value.

Soft whimpers carried along the warm breeze. Brandt turned to look in their direction. Beneath the low branch of a tree, one of his men cradled another. His chest was a bloody mess. A shaking hand rose up as if begging for help. With a long groan, he expelled his last breath and died. For the man's family, the loss was a tragedy. For Brandt, it was just another reason to hate the Russians.

The Indian - the tall American named Littlejohn - walked out of the trees and stood in the middle of the path. One of the older men raised his rifle and shouted. Brandt screamed at him in German. "Nein! Nein! Freund! Freund!"

Littlejohn walked among the ambush site, picking up the numerous brass cartridge casings from among the trees and placed them in his bag. Brandt suddenly realized he had completely forgotten to order his men to sanitize the area. He gestured for his men to do the same.

When they were all done, Littlejohn walked through the ambush site again, finding all the casings they had missed on their first run-through. Brandt was shocked. There were dozens.

Again the men scoured the site. And again Littlejohn went through and found more. The search went on a half-dozen more times before the American stopped and nodded to Brandt, who felt his face growing hotter with each pass. They did not have the time for this, but it was a necessary task if they wanted to keep their size and capabilities hidden from the enemy. Each second spent here increased the risk they would be caught. Brandt mentally noted yet another shortcoming of his men.

They needed to be faster and more efficient.

Littlejohn pulled a small black box from the burlap bag and lifted it up for Brandt to see. It was a simple device with a speaker embedded in one side and a single button on the other. A push of the button brought the speaker to life, emitting sounds that closely resembled shouting and automatic fire.

The American turned the bag over and dozens of the little devices fell out on the ground. Without pause, he planted two of them on the ground and in the branches.

Brandt almost laughed. Did the Americans think this idea would work? Sure, the devices might fool a peasant army twenty years ago, but this was 1985 Europe! Well, he would follow their advice until they were proven wrong. What else could he do?

He turned towards his men and gestured to the boxes. "Plant them. Everywhere. Go now!" The men went to work, walking deeper into the forest. When they were all turned on, a cacophony of simulated battle sounds erupted from their electronic innards. Brandt couldn't help but be amazed at the realism of the effect.

Littlejohn pulled the bulky radio from a dead Russian. He made a gesture as he dropped it in front of Brandt.

Brandt called over to his radio operator and pointed to the device. "Make the call," he said.

The young man picked up the receiver and keyed the transmit button. "Alpha Two Two to Mother, I am under attack, over. Repeat, I am under attack by an enemy force. Size undetermined. Send reinforcements immediately to grid…"

Thirty seconds later, Brandt and his men were running away from the ambush site.

Littlejohn remained near the path, watching and waiting.

The faded brick farmhouse sat on a solitary hill overlooking a patchwork of dense forest and flat countryside. Joe Ricci sat in the kitchen gazing out the window, tapping an uneven tune on the dusty old floor with his new jungle boots.

"Come on, Ned. Where are you?" he muttered.

Though it had been only a few days since he had arrived in East Germany, he had not left the house.

His work had been an exhausting litany of tasks - everything from building and maintaining the messy array of antennas in the attic to meeting with Brandt to discuss potential targets. On his rare breaks, he would sit here to take his mind off things. Slowly but surely, the myriad worries of each day would disappear in the peaceful vista. But not today.

Littlejohn was late coming back. He should have returned ten minutes ago.

If something had gone wrong, Ricci needed to know now. But how? The answer, of course, sat five feet behind him.

"Hey Jonesy!" he shouted. "You getting anything?"

No response.

He turned to see the kid sitting at the frequency scanner, wearing his bulky military-grade headphones and surfing the airwaves for enemy intel. His hand moved steadily, scribbling notes in the logbook.

The urge to go over and tap Jones on the shoulder was overruled by the fatigue caused by both age and a wartime routine. The five AM wakeups were hard enough when Joe Ricci was a twenty-year-old. It was absolute torture in his forties. He turned his attention back to the scenery in an effort to relax. Its rugged beauty was matched only by the Central Highlands of Vietnam. Though East Germany and Southeast Asia were worlds apart in almost every way, their similarities lay in their abundance of natural splendor. It was the way the wind rustled and the sunlight caught the trees just so.

The cumulative effect of all this had a way of hypnotizing people. It lulled even the most experienced operators into a false sense of security. People got careless. People got killed. It even happened to guys like Ned Littlejohn. It was one of the unspoken hazards of covert operations in enemy territory.

For the third time in less than a minute, Ricci glanced at his watch. Sitting here was not helping matters.

"Okay," Ricci said. "I need a smoke."

His yellow nicotine-stained fingers dug through the overflowing ashtray, picking out the butts until he found one with enough paper beyond the filter.

Recycled smokes, he called them. Being back in action after almost fifteen years had also brought back the nicotine habit in full force. Despite being free of the monster for the past five years, he'd brought along a few cartons of Camels on this mission because - screw it! If the world was ending, he might as well enjoy himself a little.

At last Ricci found just the right stub. Upon discovery of his prize, he flicked open the lighter only to be rewarded with a few weak sparks. The next several attempts yielded no flame either.

"Dammit!"

Ricci flung the old metal contraption across the room. It slapped against the wall and ricocheted towards the table, landing in front of Jones with a clatter. The young man jumped up from his chair and spun towards him, his eyes wide and fists clenched. "What the hell are you doin'…sir?!"

"Sorry," murmured Ricci. He took a step back and held his hands up, palms out as if in surrender.

The expression on the corporal's face softened. He placed the lighter on the table beside him then held out his own pack of cigarettes in one hand and a lighter in the other.

Ricci nodded thanks as he inhaled a lungful of tobacco. The putrid taste of menthol bit into the back of his throat as his lungs railed in protest. The world spun for a moment. He steadied himself on a nearby chair.

"They aren't back yet," said Ricci.

Jones shrugged. "Yes, sir," he said. "I know."

Ricci checked his watch. "Well, the ambush was supposed to be twenty minutes ago. Are you getting anything from the other frequencies yet?"

"No, sir," said Jones. "Just a regular day out there for the Russians right now. No wires jiggling yet."

Ricci smiled at Jones' use of the term "jiggle". He was glad to know that the jargon for listening posts hadn't changed one bit in fifteen years. It was insider language. Simply put, "jiggling the wire" meant creating a disturbance so crazy and so loud that it attracted the enemy's undivided attention.

The Russian garrison had sent out regular patrols like clockwork. The idea was to hit it as hard as possible and then simulate a request for help. When backup arrived, the simulated gunfire would create enough confusion to draw in more men. The net result would be create enough radio traffic to map the local garrison's location, capabilities, and response patterns.

"Well, keep checking," said Ricci. "Let me know when the fish are biting."

Without another word, Jones put the headphones back on and resumed punching in the times and frequencies into the printing calculator that served as a scan log. The little machine made a small whirring noise as it spat out each entry on the thick roll of paper.

Ricci stared at Jones, working away. The kid was a complete mystery. The little snippets of brief conversation they shared over the last few days earned him little insight into the young man. All Ricci had pieced together was that he was from a small town near Atlanta. Attempts to talk about sports were met with silence. When the conversation shifted over to hobbies, Jones had rattled off a list of techno-jargon that made absolutely no sense. Ricci had no interest in video games or programming so the conversation had screeched to a polite but definite halt. Sensing that the worlds they inhabited had no common foundation, both men gave up on forcing a friendship.

As the nicotine buzz wore off, a sense of calm swept over him. Taut muscles loosened like untied knots. If Jones wasn't worried, then maybe Ricci shouldn't either. He would keep himself busy until Ned came back.

Ricci finished the smoke and walked over to the table. He ripped off the sheet of paper from the calculator and began punching the numbers into the high-capacity scanner. Along with the tape cassette recorder and the logbook entries, the machine would be used to form a complete picture of the nearby enemy garrison's communications network, patrol routines, and supply situation.

Five minutes later, the manual input was completed. Ricci looked around for something else to do. Nothing jumped out, and he was not about to start cleaning.

It would have gone against one of his golden rules - listening posts should be as filthy as possible at all times.

He gave up and paced around the small kitchen, careful to lift his feet clear of the tangled nest of cords that cluttered the wooden floorboards. The house was tiny, but he had worked out of smaller places. In Laos, he had set up in caves and mud huts, which had worked just fine. The requirements for a listening post were pretty meager - some elevation, a radio, an antenna, two guys, and a logbook. Anything more than that was overkill.

Jones looked up, his bright eyes were wide and his face was creased with a grin. "I've got something," he said triumphantly. "Sounds like they're sending in the cavalry, sir."

Ricci smiled at this bit of good news. If Brandt and Ned had done their job right, the Russians back at the garrison headquarters would soon find out that one of their patrols was never coming back at all. With the help of the noisemakers, the enemy reinforcements could be in the area for hours until they uncovered the ruse. Of course, that still didn't change the fact that Ned hadn't come back.

"Okay," Ricci said. "Keep at it."

The radio operator reached for a fresh notebook from a pile of scribblers at his feet. Ricci walked over to the table and swiped the most recent entries from the top of the growing stack of completed logbooks. The Priority Three tactical reports had been filled out in neat and legible handwriting.

At the top of the page appeared the date, the operator code, time, and frequencies all written in pencil. Beneath that, the paper was divided lengthwise into two halves by a single neat line. The intercepted messages were written in Russian on the left side with the English translation on the right.

Ricci checked the frequency on Jones' radio and tapped him on the shoulder.

"128.5. That showed up yesterday too. Probably the garrison HQ. Who's talking? Archie or Reggie this time?"

Ricci always assigned pet names to the enemy radio operators, usually based on whatever classic literature he was reading at the moment.

In this case, it was the April issue of "Betty and Veronica", the tattered pages of which sat open near the sink.

Jones put the headset back on and listened for several seconds. "Archie. He talks too much. Lots of pauses."

"Yeah. Amateur hour," said Ricci. "Heavy finger on the transmit button."

From the open window, the buzz of a helicopter cut through the distant air. An Mi-8 Hip meandered over the trees far to the north, close to where Brandt's ambush had been set up. The big chopper circled lazily above the trees and halted before finally descending to the forest floor. He clucked his tongue. "So our friends have a chopper. Not good."

Ricci walked back to the radio and grabbed a Y-connector headset that let him listen to whatever Jones heard. The signal was faint but coherent enough for Ricci to pick out the confused tone of the operator's voice as he repeatedly tried to raise the patrol. Ricci spun the rotor on the wall with a surgeon's touch, slowly rotating the dipole antenna in the attic above.

Gradually, the voice on the other end became just a shade clearer and the static around the thick consonants faded. Another small turn of the antenna yielded a short spurt of static.

Ricci checked the little dial that displayed the antenna's angle. He smiled and looked at the map board on the wall. It was full of blue tacks that indicated potential contacts in the area gleaned from days of listening to local radio chatter. He pulled the blue tack from the map and replaced it with a red one. There. Now it was definite.

One more piece of the puzzle was solved. Ricci looked down at the tray of tacks on the table. If things went well enough, all the blue thumbtacks on the map would be substituted for red by the end of the day. He smiled and patted Jones on the back.

"Wittenberg," said Ricci. "Their HQ is at Wittenberg."

They would soon have enough information to start scouting enemy positions. Then they would attack, continually moving to keep the Russians off balance. Today couldn't have been more perfect. Except for one thing. Ricci looked at his watch again. Where the hell was Ned?

Now he was getting worried. Ricci's mind raced. If Ned never made it back, he would just pack it in and leave here quietly. One short encrypted radio message would bring a helicopter over here for an extraction. If Baker or Heath tried to object, Ricci would threaten to blow the whole operation. That would bring them to heel pretty quick. He helped himself to another of Jones' cigarettes.

"You hear anything from Brandt?" Ricci asked.

The regrets swarmed through his head. Ricci was supposed to go along with the insurgents to help them on their first ambush. That bit of operating procedure was killed when Brandt objected that it would make him look weak to his men. Ricci understood the logic. Every irregular organization worked the same. Authority was conferred by its members - not handed down from the top. Back at Ban Ngoc, it was the village elder who led. Ricci winced and tried to shoo away his memories of Kai's last moments, spent kneeling before a team of NVA with a rifle in his hand.

Jones stopped writing and tossed the pen on the table. He sighed and looked up. "Sorry, sir?"

"Brandt," said Ricci. "Are they in any trouble?"

The young man shrugged. "They are radio silent just like you ordered, sir."

"Look! Just call Brandt, okay?" said Ricci. This waiting around was getting ridiculous. An American operative was missing in action. Didn't anyone care about that?

Ricci held his breath while Jones keyed the small sleek digital radio that sat next to the hulking Vietnam-era equipment on the table. Jones had brought it along with him and explained that it had a kind of computer chip that handled encryption and secure transmission.

The KY-57 VINSON was supposed to be the top of the line cryptographic device. It certainly looked impressive enough. Intimidated by its array of buttons and knobs, Ricci had thrown his hands up early on and left its operation up to Jones. "I like the simple stuff," Ricci had told him.

Jones spoke a few brief words in German and tapped his cigarette on the edge of the ashtray while waiting for a reply.

When it came, he turned in his seat and announced the news with a deadpan voice, as if a plane were delayed at JFK. "They're on the way. One KIA."

A knot grew in Ricci's stomach.

"Okay, get back to scanning," he commanded.

Minutes later, the door creaked open. Ricci wheeled around. There, in the entrance stood the lanky figure of Ned Littlejohn, peering down at Ricci from dark eyes set above a beak-like nose.

Ricci laughed and ran up to shake the man's hand. "Damn you, Ned!" he said. "You sure took your time out there! I hate it when you do that."

Littlejohn stepped inside the house, maneuvering through the cramped quarters with ease. He leaned against the rusty iron stove, guzzling water from a full canteen that sat ready in the sink.

"Any luck out there?" asked Ricci. "Lemme guess - you found the entire Russian army out there and killed half of 'em. Hope you managed to leave a few for Brandt."

Littlejohn rubbed at his swollen finger. "One of Brandt's men was killed."

"How'd he die?" asked Ricci.

"He died well, Joe," Littlejohn answered.

Ricci stifled a laugh. "Let's get out of here," he said.

The men walked out of the farmhouse and into the midday heat. Ricci shielded his eyes from the sudden attack of sunlight that flooded his senses. "You're late," he said. "Everything go okay out there?"

Littlejohn nodded toward a clump of trees rustling near the edge of the clearing. Ricci held his breath, thinking of his service revolver that sat on the table beside the radio. The urge to go back in and get it was overridden by curiosity.

The man who emerged from the tree line wore an East German helmet and fatigues. In his hands, he clutched an M16. Ricci gasped as two more men appeared. It was only when Brandt walked out ahead of the group that Ricci finally realized these men were friendlies. He sat horrified at the prospect of what would have happened if he had had his weapon with him.

The platoon-sized group jogged in column formation towards the deserted barn. Four men brought up the rear, holding the edges of a full body bag. Ricci shook his head and tried not to look at it.

"We're getting good intel," said Ricci. "The kid knows his stuff."

Inside the dusty barn, the body bag sat in the center of the floor. A silent circle of men gathered around and stood at attention. Ricci had been too busy to notice them before, but now he could see what a motley group they were. Some of them were broad-shouldered men with the bodies of laborers. Others looked like they would have fit right in behind a desk in a New York skyscraper. Some wore faces filled with apprehension and fear while others seemed grim and determined.

Brandt walked into the circle and stood by the body. He scanned the faces of each man, his eyes halting on Ricci and Littlejohn. When he finally spoke, the words came out in English instead of German.

"Today, we were bloodied in combat. You all performed your jobs well. I am very proud of you," he said. "This man died for the sake of his country's future so that one day perhaps our children will live in a better society. Now that we have suffered and bled and killed, some of you may harbor doubts. Stay strong! I assure you - more hardships await. Others will die. But the dream for a better tomorrow lives on."

The men bowed their heads in silence. A minute passed. Then a buzz of activity commenced. Some of the East Germans cleaned their weapons while others smoked and chatted. Brandt walked straight towards where Ricci and Littlejohn stood.

"Let's talk," he said. The three men stepped outside into the warm sunlight.

Brandt took big gulps from Littlejohn's canteen then poured the rest over his head.

"Do you know what happened today? We killed them. Every single one. Everything went perfectly," Brandt said. "I thought they would be much tougher."

"Those are the Russians in your backyard," said Ricci. "They're from a Category C division. Bottom of the barrel."

"Yes. Yes," said Brandt. "I understand all that. We've eliminated a patrol now. What next? You're advisers. What do you advise?"

Ricci pointed to the farmhouse. "Let me show you something."

Inside the cramped kitchen, Ricci pointed to the map on the wall as Jones placed yet another red pin on it. "At first glance, you didn't do all that much. But two things happened today that will help us out. First of all, you got bloodied. For the rest of their lives, your men will share a bond that will be stronger than their differences in ideology. I'm willing to believe that if we had held on for another day or so, the cracks would have gotten too big." Ricci paused. "Hopefully, that alone will help stem your desertion problems."

Brandt cast his eyes at the floor. "And the second?" he asked.

"We got a ton of intel," said Ricci. "We know where the garrison is. Tonight, we'll send out a recon team to take a closer look. That's something you can tell your men. They'll need to know what they bought with their sweat and blood today. Get 'em rested up, Brandt. But keep them busy too. Lots of chores. Lots of light duties."

Brandt nodded. "Everything I thought would be easy was difficult," he said. "And everything that seemed so difficult was quite easy. All we did was wait for them and then pull the trigger."

Ricci chuckled. "That's the way it is. You get used to it."

"And I lost a man today," said Brandt, taking in a deep lungful of smoke. "I ask myself, 'What went wrong? What should I have done instead?'"

"That - you never get used to," Ricci answered. "But if you keep asking yourself that, you'll go crazy. At least you're reacting to it. That's a good sign. Ned and me - we served under a couple of officers back in 'Nam who didn't care how many of us died. All that mattered was the mission - higher body counts. More death. It got us nowhere."

"So what's the plan then?" asked Brandt. "After we hit the garrison. Then what?"

"Then we'll have free rein to hit the Russian reinforcements as they come down the road," said Ricci. "But let's not get too far ahead of ourselves yet. First thing's first. We need to take a look at the garrison HQ."

"Fine," said Brandt as he rubbed his hands. "Let's not waste any time."

Ricci watched him leave and then looked at Littlejohn. "That guy scares me," he said.

Littlejohn rubbed at the swollen injury on his finger. He looked up at Ricci.

"Me too."

HERE I STAND

Wittenberg, East Germany
Coswigerstrasse
May 9, 1985

Littlejohn beckoned the two men over to the window and pointed south. The tall spiked dome of the castle church towered over the city like a sentinel. Below it sat the rows of barbed wire and the metal fence where soldiers patrolled around the perimeter of the All Saints Church.

He passed the starlight scope to the two young men and leaned back away from the window, listening to the jet fighters streak across the sky. Occasionally, an explosion could be heard off in the distance. Everywhere around them was pure destruction - everywhere except for this pristine place.

Below where he sat, Littlejohn heard the rumble of an engine and he poked his head just over the window sill. An armored vehicle passed through the narrow street below him. It had eight large tires and a small turret with a machine gun mounted from the inside. Like any good scout, Littlejohn had done his homework before coming over here. He knew most of the Russian equipment by sight. This was a BTR-60. Inside its belly was a Russian patrol on its way back to base.

He mentally noted the time and nodded to the two men beside him as the gate around the church opened. The vehicle passed beyond the fence and into the nearby park where it halted near a clump of bushes.

Twelve passengers emerged from the rear doors then milled around, talking loudly and smoking cigarettes. Littlejohn pushed two buttons on the tape recorder. A series of small LEDs on the top of the machine blinked, which confirmed that the careless chatter was being captured on tape. Later, Jones and the East Germans would listen for anything of value and use it to plan future attacks.

Littlejohn picked up the pencil once again and completed his sketch of the area on a small notepad. Carefully drawn arrows pointed out the weak spots and vulnerabilities of the church and its surroundings. The men with him were tasked with watching and writing down anything of note then marking the time beside it.

Ned already saw the mistakes. The garrison commander had set patrols around the perimeter that never varied. The corners of the buildings had blind spots which were left uncovered by sentries or machine gun nests. The countless trees in the park hadn't been cut down and offered an abundance of cover and concealment.

Still, the place was built as a fortress. Even an amateur tactician could still manage to hold against a determined assault.

A hundred braves who had already embraced their deaths might find their way in, kill plenty of enemies, and destroy the old church. Thirty new fighters who had barely won their first battle - that was another matter entirely.

That would leave it up to the airplanes to destroy. Joe would place the call. The planes would come in and destroy everything. Nothing would be left.

A shrill cry rang out in the night. Ned's brain snapped back to the here and now. There it was again - muffled but unmistakable. An infant unleashed its hungry howl for the world to hear. Littlejohn's heart hammered in his chest as he realized there were innocents here.

Suddenly, the prospect of a NATO air strike took on a much darker tone in his head. Visions of an Arc Light B-52 strike danced in his mind. It was August 1970. He was sitting on a hill watching the far-off jungle tremble and shake and explode again and again.

He hadn't seen any signs of life in the town all night. They had made their way from the outskirts to the city center by passing through a series of abandoned buildings and homes. Joe had guessed that the entire population had been moved back east to make room for the constant stream of Russians who were passing through the area. He was wrong.

One of Brandt's men stared at Littlejohn as the baby cried out again in the dark. Littlejohn gestured towards the doorway. Ten minutes later, the town of Wittenberg was behind them.

REFORMATION

Ricci slapped a hand on the wooden table. "Not gonna happen," he said.

Brandt pointed to the hand-drawn sketches and raised his voice. "It must be done! There is no other way!"

The East German major lit a cigarette with the flame of the kerosene lamp and stared down at the shed's dirty floor. "You underestimate us," he grumbled. "We go in there, and we strike them fast and hard. Wipe them out."

What would it take to make this American understand? The Russians were in Wittenberg. They would use the element of surprise to shock them with an audacious attack straight at their headquarters. He and his men would cut off the head of the snake and watch the body die.

Ricci hooked his thumb towards Littlejohn and sighed. "This thing is heavily fortified. To top it off, we have reason to believe civilians are living right around there. If we go in there with guns blazing, your people die and those civilians die. End of story!"

Brandt picked up the sketches that the American had made and looked again at them. They were drawn with the skill of a real artist. The pencil lines showed the brash arcs of the centuries-old church. He could even make out the 95 Theses that had been nailed to its doors centuries ago.

In no way did he wish to harm such a place of history and culture in his own country - but there was no other choice. It was now an enemy stronghold. Whatever sentimental value it held for the German people was now perverted and sullied at the hands of the invaders. The blame for its destruction would lay squarely at the feet of the Russians.

"We need to stick with the plan and keep hitting them where it hurts," said Ricci. "We drain their supplies, sap their will to fight, and take out their key assets. Then we hit the headquarters. Until then, you're looking at a suicide mission. Besides - I thought you wanted to liberate your country, not destroy it."

Brandt's mind raced. The American's objections centered on two essential details - the church fortress and the civilians. Which was the real problem?

"Mr. Ricci, you have me confused with an idealist," said Brandt. "In this country, those kinds of people don't live very long." He wanted to sit down with the American, explain to him how he had spent his life compromising to get his revenge.

Brandt had struggled for years to ingratiate himself to a system that he hated from the moment he watched his father bleed out on the street all for the sake of an extra two marks a week. The lesson was the first one he had learned in his life - ideals were mutable but bitter hatred could never change. It was the only thing that got him through each day.

Ricci sighed. "I understand you want the Russians out of here. We do too. But a suicide attack isn't going to work. Neither will raining down bombs on the place and hoping for the best."

"I thought your weapons were precision-guided?" said Brandt. He remembered reading the intelligence briefings on NATO's newest "smart" weapons. They had caused considerable alarm and confusion among the Warsaw Pact's military leaders. Why worry about how exact a weapon could be when you could just make its effects so big that it could never miss? The idea of avoiding so-called collateral damage seemed foolhardy and vain. War was war and always would be.

"Well, that's true," said Ricci. "I don't really know enough about them these days. But from what I saw over in Vietnam and Laos, precision bombing was pretty far from precise. No. Sorry, I'm not gonna risk it. Request denied."

Brandt threw his hands up. "Well then, Mr. Ricci. It appears we have reached an impasse. I will not follow your advice, and you will not assist me. It seems that our relationship is at an end." It was time to see how far the leash extended. Would the American call his bluff?

Ricci folded his arms together. "I agree. We'll be pulling out of here tomorrow morning. The weapons and supplies already provided by my government are yours to keep. The other stuff," he pointed to the radio equipment, "we'll be taking back with us." Ricci extended a hand. Brandt took it, trying to hide his astonishment at how wrong he had been. It seemed the Americans had honestly wanted to help out.

Brandt kept his head down, astonished at how badly he had misjudged Ricci. He searched for something to say, but the cards were already on the table. Nothing could bring back what had happened. "Good luck, Captain Ricci. Thank you for your valuable assistance," he said. He shook Littlejohn's hand and sat back down.

Ricci collected the sketches from the table. "It was our pleasure, Major Brandt. We'll be busy packing up tonight. Don't mind us."

Brandt got up from the table and strolled towards the door, wondering at his stillborn revolution. How long would his current supplies last until they ran out? A week - maybe less, he figured. He would soon face a full-scale mutiny without equipment and food. Well, that was it. He would wait for the Americans to leave and then disband the group of fighters. It was the only way.

As his hand fell on the rusty doorknob, a shout welled up in the night. The drumbeat of frantic footsteps grew louder. A terrified young man threw open the door. His eyes were wide, and his voice trembled.

"Sir!" he shouted. "One of our men was caught at the perimeter trying to sneak away! We have him in the barn. He's talking. Sir, I believe he's a traitor!"

"Fine work," said Brandt. "I'll be right there. Do not harm the man. I want to talk to him."

Brandt stared at Ricci. "Help me," he murmured. "Please. Help me, Joe."

FLANK HITS

In the center of the barn were two men. One stood with a gun in his hand while the other knelt, his hands tied behind his back and a bruised face smeared with blood. The man holding the pistol glanced at Ricci then delivered a swift kick to the captive's stomach. With a grunt, he collapsed onto the dusty wooden floor. A chest walled by broken ribs swelled as the man gasped for air.

"Brandt, make him stop," said Ricci.

"Halt!" shouted Brandt. "I want this man moved to the shed immediately. The rest of you will stay here and wait for further orders. Ready your gear. Be prepared to move."

Minutes later, the four men sat in the cramped shed. Ricci sat across from the young captive, staring at his swollen and battered visage.

"You get one chance and one chance only," said Ricci. The words came out slow and calm - almost at a whisper. There was no mistaking the deadly intent behind them. He had used it countless times with the Viet Cong and the NVA soldiers they had captured. The soothing tone threw them off guard and usually got them talking pretty quickly.

The young man stared at the desk, averting Ricci's gaze.

"Where were you going? What were you planning to do? Answer in English."

"I…I was going to meet with someone," he said. The words came out haltingly, each consonant quavering.

"Who?"

Ricci laid his service revolver on the table, the barrel pointing towards the man.

"I am NOT going to ask again."

No reply. Ricci hooked a thumb at Ned.

"Do you see this man behind me, son? You're looking at a full-blooded Comanche Indian. Do you know what they do to prisoners? They skin them alive. I've seen it. How long do you think you can live without your skin, sitting there in agony you can't even imagine? You'd want to scream over and over again. But you couldn't. Because the first thing Mr. Littlejohn will do is cut your tongue out." Ricci waited a beat and then added. "Still want to keep quiet?"

The young man looked up at Littlejohn. His eyes were wide and his body shook. Like a rough tide in a storm, his stomach heaved and settled.

Ricci shook his head slowly. "I was afraid you'd try and be brave. Ah well. Ned? Go to work."

Littlejohn stepped forward and grabbed the hilt of the long knife sheathed in the leather scabbard tied to his waist. The blade inched its way upwards, the sheen of sharp polished metal reflecting the flame of the kerosene lamp. As the knife inched upward, Littlejohn shut his eyes tight and chanted in tongues. The sweat poured from the young man's face as his breathing grew rapid. When Littlejohn finally pulled the blade free, the captive was convulsing, his jaw chattering and tears forming in his eyes.

"I'll talk!" he said. "I'll tell you!"

Ricci stepped forward as Littlejohn continued with his chant. "You tell me everything right now!" shouted Ricci.

"I spoke to the Russians," said the young man, the words falling out so rapid that Ricci nearly had to ask him again.

"The Russians?! They know where we are? Where are they?"

"They're coming!" said the young man. "They're going to attack!"

Ricci grabbed the captive by the collar and leaned in close. The stench of the man's barely-contained panic filled the air between them.

"When? When are they attacking?"

"Soon! Very soon!" he said. "They're everywhere! They have us surrounded!"

Ricci's gut dropped. He turned to Littlejohn. "Warn the others! Now!"

His friend sheathed the knife and ran out of the shed. Ricci turned to Brandt.

"Rally point?"

The major shook his head. "The men were briefed on the rally point. We have to assume it's compromised. I know another place though." He pointed to the young captive. "What should be done with him?"

Ricci handed the Makarov over to Brandt. "This piece of crap? Do whatever you want, major."

Ricci ran out of the shed just before the shot rang out. Inside the farmhouse, he kicked at the sleeping figure of Corporal Jones.

"Get everything packed," he shouted. "We gotta get the hell out of here. Come on! Move!"

Ricci's head reeled, trying to consider ways of escaping the trap.

Jones stirred and groaned then got busy packing up the scanner. Ricci grabbed the logbooks, his hands shaking as he tried to shove them into his pack. One of the books fell from his grip and lay open on the floor. Its pages contained meticulous details of frequencies and conversations printed neatly in Russian and English. He glanced over at the map board full of red pins and saw that Jones still hadn't started packing up the VINSON.

"Jonesy! I got a job for you," he said. "I want you to get on their company net and spoof 'em. Say there's an attack on the south side of the hill and request assistance. Then I want you to send out a call to their regimental artillery group. See if you can get hold of a battery commander." Ricci held up the logbook to the page number that held the enemy codes and frequencies. "Tell them the grid co-ordinates for the south end of the hill and order time on target fire support. Open SHEAF. You think you can do that?"

Corporal Jones beamed. "Call down an artillery strike on their own guys? I like your way of thinking, sir." He sat down at the desk and dialed in the radio settings.

"When you're done with that, I want you to grab whatever you can carry and forget the rest," said Ricci as he placed a pair of white phosphorous grenades next to the young man. "Then toss these in the door and run like hell. We'll be waiting for you on the north side of the perimeter."

Jones nodded as he got to work, flipping through the logbooks and speaking in rapid-fire Russian on the radio.

Ricci jogged out the door and into the middle of the clearing. Most of the East Germans were already there with their weapons and packs on. Brandt and Littlejohn approached.

"Are we ready to go yet?" asked Ricci.

Brandt nodded. "We're ready to fight our way out."

"Hopefully that won't be necessary," said Ricci. "You got any of those noisemakers left, Ned?"

"Yeah, Joe." Littlejohn patted his burlap bag.

Ricci smiled. "Turn 'em on and toss 'em out on the south side of the perimeter as far as you can throw them. Don't worry about anything fancy. Just throw and get back here as fast as you can! Then we head north." Littlejohn ran off into the darkness.

Ricci checked his watch. Three thirty in the morning. A perfect time to attack. As a way to give the exhausted men a little respite, he had ordered the patrols halved. He had gotten lazy with perimeter security and now they were all going to pay. These were usually the kinds of mistakes you only made once. His heart thumped as he guided the men towards the north side of the clearing.

All around them, the Russians were closing in fast with deadly intent. Now he was outnumbered and on the run with the enemy at an advantage. All because of one man. How many more informants were in their midst?

Ten seconds later, the first gunshot rang out. Ricci smiled as the south side of the hill erupted in automatic weapons fire. Littlejohn sprinted out of the darkness towards them.

The trees near the south side of the perimeter lit up, and a half-dozen figures poured out of them.

The covering fire sprayed everywhere in wild fully-automatic bursts. Ricci crouched low and shot at the nearest of the men while Brandt's followers fanned out and returned fire. A tracer bit into the air above Ricci's head and someone behind him screamed. He fell prone and began crawling away from the enemy as the chaos and confusion around him mounted.

Littlejohn brushed past, firing single shots as he moved. Ricci caught the flash of an enemy's muzzle and fired back in its direction with a tight three-round burst. Brandt's machine gun team opened up with the M60, sending tight disciplined shots into the tree line.

Ricci hurled hand grenades at the Russians in the open while 40mm grenade rounds silenced the rest of the Russian fire base. The hole in the enemy line had been made. Now it was time to punch through before it closed. Ricci stood up on legs that trembled and trotted over the fresh bodies and into the trees.

In the darkness of the forest, Ricci rested against a tree and looked back at the burning farmhouse. Did Jones make it out of there or had the Russians gotten him first? It was impossible to tell from here.

A gale-force wind swept over his head like a freight train. The south side of the hill leapt up as a series of explosions hammered down on it. The ground recoiled with the impact of 75mm shells raining down on the enemy's own position. A lone figure sprinted towards them. Ricci hollered and waved his hands, hoping the corporal would know where to run in the darkness.

Brandt ran up to Ricci, his face streaked with tension. "We have to move! Follow close!"

Down the hill and through the thick forest, they scrambled in the dark. Ricci tried hard to keep up with Littlejohn's long effortless strides. Artillery splashed down in the distance. Ricci looked back to see the hillside consumed by a raging inferno that lit up the night sky.

An acrid and evil smell wafted through the wind, choking Ricci until his lungs ached and his legs refused to move. Ricci leaned against a tree and took huge gulping breaths. By the time he finally found his legs again, everyone else was gone. The terror of black solitude rendered his body immobile.

Staying here seemed to be a huge mistake but moving anywhere was somehow even worse. He had been lost in the jungle so many times and made his way out fine. He was young back then and his body was a finely tuned machine. Now, he was just a dumpy middle-aged guy with a paunch and a desk job. Who the hell did he think he was fooling, coming all the way out here and playing soldier?

The crunch of boots on leaves seemed to come from multiple directions. He took a tentative step forward then paused to peer through the inky blackness that swarmed all around him. He counted the seconds, balling his hands into fists in a vain attempt to keep the terror at bay. All the while, his friends were moving further and further away from him. Streaks of sweat cascaded down his back.

A strange epiphany swept over him. In a sudden moment of clarity, he realized what it must have been like for Baker all those years ago. Suddenly, he understood the resentment just beneath the man's words at the briefing. Ricci had left him for dead. The man had spent three days and nights alone in a hostile land just like this, praying each minute that he would see his family again.

When Baker had returned to base, the man had joked about the ordeal with Ricci, who was never brave enough to probe beyond the laughter into the pain and anger underneath it. Despite all that, the man he had abandoned in the jungle had thought of Ricci and Ned when the time came and gave him this opportunity.

There was no list of possible candidates for this mission. Baker had known all along that Ricci's wife was dead. He knew damn well that Ned was a recovered junkie living on the fringes of society. At their lowest points, Baker had reunited them like long lost brothers. In return, Ricci had treated Baker shabbily and embarrassed him in front of Heath.

Mosquitoes swarmed around his skin. Every so often, one of them would land on an exposed part of his body and venture a taste of his blood. What the memories had done to his sense of self all these long years, the bugs were now doing to his blood. They took and took without ever returning. Ricci slapped at his left forearm.

No sooner had the painful itch halted than it resumed once again - this time on his right ankle. This is how he would spend the night.

Once morning arrived, he would find a place where he could see the hillside to orient himself. Then he would find shelter and sleep through the day. He was in the middle of a vast forest and possessed enough survival skills to live here if need be. The area was rich in water and food, with its countless streams and wildlife. He would pass the days alone until the war was over and he could surrender to whoever was in control of this turf.

Ricci cursed at the thought.

Who was he kidding?

Alone and scared and with no reason to continue living, he would find a way to take his own life. Ricci would not spend weeks crapping in the bush only to be followed by years spent doing hard labor in a Russian concentration camp. There was just no way. His hand wandered towards the pistol in his waistband as he fought against the choking shroud of despair that descended over him.

Ricci hesitated and closed his eyes and remembered his wife and her beautiful face on the day he first met her. Then came the image of the little streak of premature gray that crept up on her as she turned thirty-five and they had finally given up on having children. He recalled the withered husk that cancer had left behind after it ravaged her body. Through it all, she had fought every battle like a lion. A tear came to Ricci's eye.

And what had Ricci done to help her win? Nothing. Instead, he had volunteered for a desk job going through cold cases so he didn't have to face visiting her in the hospital every night. The despair chipped away at his soul. How easy it was to betray those who had deserved it the least. Knowing that they would forgive it all made the deed so much more sinister.

His hand relaxed as he took on the unspoken debt and promised to repay it. Somewhere out there someone needed his help and he would give it freely and without expectation of anything in return. It was the only way to salvation. He had to live, if only for someone else.

Ricci stepped forward into the darkness.

And fell.

He tumbled down the steep drop, his body slapping back and forth among the trees like a pinball on a high score run.

When he finally stopped, he lay there in the cool night air and counted the fresh aches all over his body. Then Ricci opened his eyes and looked up through the canopy of trees to see the dim stars laid out in the purple pre-dawn sky. Slowly, his thoughts coalesced. It would be light soon. He would stay put until someone found him. There it was.

Somewhere nearby, the leaves crunched. A twig snapped.

Ricci reached for his M16 and lifted it to his shoulder, straining to see into the gloom.

Two men strode through the darkness, their rifles at the ready. They were close enough to make out their faces. One of them looked very young - no older than a high school freshman. The other had graying hair and shouted at Ricci in Russian and German. With his M16 raised to his shoulder, Ricci pulled the trigger. Nothing.

Before either man could react, the end of a long blade protruded through the older man's chest.

His stomach heaved as the man screamed and writhed on his way to the ground. Behind where he stood was Ned Littlejohn, a long bloody knife in his hand. The young man next to him stepped back and threw his weapon to the ground with a clatter. Three backward steps brought his back against a tree trunk. Littlejohn would make short work of him if no one put a stop to it.

Ricci's hand shot up. "Ned. He's just a kid."

Littlejohn halted in his stride. His hands clutched the knife, poised to sink into the young man's throat.

Ricci plucked the kid's weapon from the ground and turned it over in his hands. His palm swept over the beautiful finish of the Mosin-Nagant. Where had it been? Ricci imagined long winter days spent in the arms of men whose only goal was to push the Germans back from Stalingrad inch by bloody inch all the way to Berlin.

The romantic notions in his mind screeched to a halt when he checked the bolt.

It was filthy. Ricci couldn't help but feel a kind of indignity on the weapon's behalf.

Ned turned the boy around and searched him. Halfway through the ordeal, the young man wheezed out a childish sob. When it was over, Ricci rolled his eyes and slung the Russian rifles over his shoulder then cleared the jam from his own rifle.

"Let's go," said Ricci. "Let's find Brandt."

Littlejohn used a roll of twine to tie the teenager's hands behind his back then blindfolded him by winding a roll of medical gauze around his head. With one hand on the kid's shoulder, Littlejohn turned to Ricci. "Follow me," he said.

Twenty minutes later, they were home - or something that resembled it.

RESURRECTION

Brandt woke from a dreamless sleep. Exhaustion still gnawed at the corners of his mind. The haggard face and matching scowl of the man who stood over him came into focus. It was "Twenty Three", the leader of second squad - his best men. The American rifle was cradled in the man's arms. His lips were pursed tight around a lit cigarette.

Brandt took a sharp breath and stared back up at him, exposed and defenseless. The thought slithered into his pulsing head. Was this a messenger or an executioner?

"Sir, the Americans are here," said Twenty Three. "They've brought a prisoner." The squad leader walked out of the cave. Brandt lay there alone, summoning the will to stand. At last, he rose shakily from the ground. The top of his head banged hard against the rocky ceiling. After the stars subsided, he ducked down and shuffled towards the light of the entrance. His steps echoed through the chamber as he ran a finger along the cold stone walls and remembered when he came here to hike during happier times.

Though they were shallow, the tight grouping of little caves had offered a natural shelter from the springtime downpours. The nearby waterfall was the perfect place for a bath or a pleasant drink. It was a small world of its own that gave a temporary escape from the hard life of a junior infantry officer. Now it was a refuge from a genuine enemy that wanted him dead.

Brandt emerged to see the three Americans in the middle of the ravine. The East German survivors of last night's ordeal - twenty-seven in all - sat in a semi-circle, saying nothing. Their attention was fixed on the terrified young prisoner who knelt down in the center. A white gauze bandage was wrapped tightly around his face to serve as a makeshift blindfold.

"Talk," said Ricci.

The man spoke in a stream of panicked Russian. Even Brandt couldn't follow the prisoner's thoughts, which seemed to be pouring out all at once.

Jones shook his head after several false starts at translation. "You need to calm this guy down, sir," he told Ricci. "I can't get anything out of him."

The American captain removed the blindfold and offered up some chocolate and a pack of cigarettes. The prisoner's face twisted. A shiver of contempt ran through Brandt, who stood listening to the interrogation with his arms folded. By the time the prisoner was finished talking, they had very little information of use.

Jones announced what Brandt had already figured out.

"He came from a collective farm in Kazakh. The KGB came and took him away a few weeks ago. They gave him a moth-eaten uniform and threw him on a train. He doesn't know much about the garrison. First, he says it's a hundred guys, then eighty, then seventy. Either this guy's not very bright or he's telling us what he thinks we want to hear, sir."

"You are treating him like a child," Brandt complained. "Let my men have some time with him. We can find out the information you need."

Ricci shook his head. "He likely doesn't know anything. But that's okay. Sometimes the important information you get from interrogation isn't from the answers themselves. It's how the questions are answered. The whole idea is to get a sample of what you're dealing with."

Brandt shrugged. "All you need to know is that he is Russian scum. I will shoot him as soon as you leave." Leave. The word rang like a bell in his head, conjuring the memories of the previous night. He had gambled on Ricci's acquiescence to the plan to assault the headquarters - and lost. Soon the Americans would depart.

Brandt looked around at his men who sat on the nearby rocks. Their faces were drawn tight with exhaustion. Still, they went about their daily routines, cleaning their rifles and sorting their kit. The awkward silences that marked the first days of training had given way to camaraderie. They joked quietly with each other, shared cigarettes, and replaced bandages on each other's wounds. Despite the hell of last night, these men were anything but defeated.

How would he meet them and tell them that the Americans were leaving and that they no longer had the supplies to go on? Was he man enough to face them and admit that his stubbornness had been the principal cause of it? Brandt was getting older. He had no children. No legacy. Only this.

Ricci sighed and shook his head. "Yeah, you're right, Brandt. Do whatever you want with him then. Jones! Get on the horn. Let 'em know we're coming home. This goose is cooked."

"Captain Ricci, I believe the situation has changed since last night," said Brandt. His pride sunk like an anchor. "It seems we have lost the element of surprise - for now. It may be that your tactics are necessary for the time being. I'll give you a chance to demonstrate their effectiveness."

Ricci nodded. "If you can't stand the heat, get out of the kitchen."

Brant tried to piece together the meaning in his head then gave up. "I don't quite follow."

"It means we're gonna go make life so hard for them, they'll either die or get out of here." Ricci pulled out the map and showed it to the captive. "Jones, I want to know if this kid knows where the garrison gets its supplies from."

The young corporal began conversing in flawless Russian then paused. "He doesn't know the map at all. But he's driven the trucks once or twice. They go up to an airbase near here. He says it's a big airfield. Lots of large aircraft. The biggest he's ever seen before."

Brandt plucked the map from Jones' hands. He scanned the contours and names until he spotted it. "There it is. Sperenberg. Thirty five kilometers northeast of here."

Ricci looked at the map then back at Jones. "Way out of our operating area," he said. "We've got lots to talk about. I need to know about that fancy radio of yours, Jones."

Brandt felt the doom-filled clouds part for the first time. He looked around at the men who were ready to continue the fight. So this was what it was like to have a family.

By dusk, they were moving together through the woods.

It had been two long frantic nights of marching through the countryside in the dark, belly crawling through the thickets and slipping through areas patrolled by men and armored vehicles. At one point, they got into a confused firefight. The enemy tracers streamed over Brandt's head as he and his men fired back and scrambled away into the darkness.

No one was hurt, but the chaos out in the countryside had caught them off guard. It was a reminder that the war itself had its own way of sculpting the environment. Despite all their plans and agendas, the gods laughed back in their faces. Everywhere, there were signs of things starting to fall apart. East Germany was teetering on the brink of anarchy. A week's worth of war had begun to slice at the delicate threads that held society together.

So be it, Brandt thought, as he wandered the burning wastes. They would burn out the enemy and rebuild the country again - just like in the last war. Only this time, they would do it without Russian meddling.

The night was lit by a long column of burning supply trucks. Fighter jets sliced through the air above, dropping their ordnance on targets further east. A wall of flame ran along the eastern horizon as the distant explosions blossomed upward from the ground.

The scarlet sky was like a seductress - sublime and deadly with the temptation to give in to the random death and unleashed chaos that scarred the land.

Brandt felt the bloodlust rising within. How dearly he wanted to kill the Russians. To rip the heart out of each of them. The ambush did not satiate the desire. Instead, it had only left him wanting more.

When they finally arrived near the airbase, Brandt and his second squad slithered through the large open field, slipping through two patrols in the darkness. Littlejohn had taken temporary command and shuffled the men around before going towards the base with a small surveillance team in tow. Without anyone accompanying him, Brandt felt stupid and useless as he lay in the tall grass alone. He let out a long impatient breath and crawled towards his men.

Nervous guard dogs inside the fence let off occasional yelps. The engines of BMP armored vehicles rumbled off in the distance. The Russians had taken the airbase security quite seriously. It was amazing they had not mined the fallow field where he and his men now lay. Such a thought made Brandt freeze up.

Less than two hundred meters away sat Sperenberg airbase, a major military transport hub for the Warsaw Pact. Anything that was vital to the war against the capitalists came through there. Of course, attacking the place with thirty men was suicide - but there were alternatives. The Americans had tried to explain the plan to Brandt, but something was lost in the translation. Ricci had finally given up. "Ned will show you," he said. But they had no mortars, no air support, and no artillery. Skeptical was not a strong enough word to describe Brandt's feelings about what they were doing.

Just as one of the transport plane's engines screamed low overhead, Brandt covered the final distance to the surveillance team. Two of his men lay prone beside Littlejohn. The American passed a pair of night vision goggles over to them. Brandt could only wonder what they revealed. The entire facility was shrouded in blackout darkness - a half-hearted attempt to throw off NATO jets and bombers.

After a minute, Brandt got hold of the goggles and held them up to see for himself. The world before him turned a hundred shades of green. Suddenly, everything in front of him was visible. There was the chain-linked fence topped with barbed wire.

Beyond that were the massive four-engine aircraft lined up on the tarmac. In the middle of the runway, repair crews and vehicles worked to fix the damage from NATO bombs. What looked like an entire regiment of surface-to-air missile vehicles were interspersed with anti-aircraft guns throughout the airport's flat expanse.

Littlejohn extended an arm in front of his face and poked his thumb upwards. He brandished his notebook and, like an artist painting a portrait, Littlejohn drew out the rough sketch of the base with measurements included. On a separate page, he drew the tall wiry form of an antenna near the control tower, taking careful note of its height.

Brandt sat frozen in riveted suspense as if he were watching a magic trick being performed.

Littlejohn dug through his pack and pulled out a box-like device with a digital readout and a host of switches. He put a hand over the screen as it lit up. Brandt recognized it as a frequency counter from Ricci's mission briefing back at the caves earlier.

"What now?" whispered Brandt. "Do we attack?"

Littlejohn pushed a few buttons and then watched the screen for a few seconds as the numbers climbed upwards. Brandt lay in the grass, too enthralled to swat at the insects that floated around his face. When the machine stopped counting, Littlejohn pushed a button and slid it back into his burlap bag.

"We go back," said Ned.

Brandt grit his teeth and followed the rest of his men back through the field. Crawling on their bellies, they covered the flat distance until they reached the cover of a forest. Brandt crouched and waited until he could see the shapes and forms of the other men.

After five minutes spent getting into formation, they picked and stumbled their way over the rocks and stumps and thick vegetation. By the time they reached the clearing, Brandt had only fallen on his face twice.

Despite his wish to complain and feel sorry for himself, he knew he was getting better at moving in the dark.

Brandt performed a quick head count and confirmed that everyone was still there - a welcome relief from the usual task of having to go back through the trees and find the stragglers. Then the trek began anew. This time it was a punishing uphill walk through the dense vegetation.

Flies swarmed in his face and bats swooped just above their heads. As they climbed the long slope, the first few rays of sunlight poked gingerly through the trees. Brandt's legs ached, and his lungs screamed for a break. By the time they found the summit, he felt like he had arrived at the top of Mount Everest.

Crowned by a line of majestic tall pines, the top of the tall hill was little more than a grassy patch of land. In the middle of it, sat a large green tent with a long whip-like antenna poking out at the top. Ricci and Jones sat inside working together at the radio. Brandt collapsed on the ground, his calves grateful for the respite.

Littlejohn fished out the frequency scanner from his bag and tossed it to Jones, who turned it on and grinned. The American radio expert's fingers danced over the dials on the blinking metal contraption that sat on the card table. Its plastic surface bowed precariously under the weight of the machines. There was a high-pitched squeal, a burst of static, and then suddenly - a voice. Faint at first, it grew loud and clear as the American corporal plucked at a knob on the machine.

"Bird Two Two. Come to angels four. Heading two nine zero," it said.

Ricci smiled. "That's it. Nice work."

Brandt folded his arms. "I still don't really understand what is happening here. We aren't attacking the airbase. We aren't disabling its transmitters. Are we listening to planes coming in? We can see that from up here ourselves." He pointed up as a heavy transport plane howled overhead. The water-filled plastic cup on the card table shook and fell over as the aircraft lumbered through the skies. "There's one," he said.

"Oh, non-believer," said Ricci. "Jones and I have been up practicing our lines for the last three hours. Just you wait and see."

He flipped a series of switches and counted down quietly with his fingers. Three. Two. One.

The VINSON let out a short burst of loud buzzing static followed by a weightless silence.

"They're cut," Ricci said. He counted again with his fingers. When he reached one, he nodded to Jones. "Showtime."

The young man's voice cracked. "Bird Two Two. Uh…"

Ricci's eyes went wide. He nodded and motioned for Jones to continue talking.

"Bird Two Two. Come to angels two. Heading two eight two," he said.

The voice on the other end came back again. "Angels Five. Two Eight Two. Confirm."

Ten seconds later, Jones spoke again. "Red Star Eight One. Come to angels five. Maintain heading."

Ricci grabbed the calculator off the table and started jotting numbers in the notebook. Brandt craned his neck to see what exactly he was writing, but it seemed a mess of trigonometry that he had not studied since grade school.

"What are you doing?" asked Brandt.

Ricci looked up from the notebook. "Why don't you go outside and find out?"

The sun was low over the horizon, spreading its lazy golden blanket out over the nearby trees and farmland. From here, Brandt had a more or less unobstructed view of Sperenberg as dawn broke. Above the base, an Ilyushin Il-76 banked in a lazy circle across the sky. Even from here, the plane looked massive. How could something so large manage to fly in the air?

Brandt had been in the military for a long time. He knew these aircraft were valuable workhorses of the Soviet Air Force. The cargo cabins could hold a company of paratroopers or three air assault vehicles or enough supplies to keep a regiment moving and fighting for days. The aircraft was in high demand by all the services; whatever they carried was top priority. To the north of the base, he made out another one of the large transport planes as it banked gently and ascended to maintain its flight pattern over Sperenberg.

The plane to the south made its own turn a second later, its nose dipping down in a gradual descent. Brandt looked on, the full realization of what was about to happen dawned on him.

The pilot in the plane to the north of the airfield saw it first. The hulking transport made a sharp turn. Its starboard wing was nearly ninety degrees to the ground when the other aircraft's nose lifted up in a bid to avoid the collision. It was all far too late.

The port wing of the southern aircraft clipped the nose of the other Ilyushin. One of the planes spun on its long axis as its rear stabilizer sheared through the belly of the other airplane. Metal fragments spewed outward and both aircraft tumbled towards the tarmac, locked in a fatal embrace. A tremendous fireball erupted from the impact point. Smoke and dust heaved upwards into the morning sky. The shockwave rippled from the epicenter, shaking the low buildings. Moments later, the entire airbase was ablaze. The flames from the burning jet fuel spewed over the long line of aircraft sitting near the runway.

He felt a tap on his shoulder and whirled around. Ricci stood there, pointing down at the burning enemy airbase.

"Major Brandt, you wanted to kill Russians. I wanted to cut off their supplies. This morning, we did both. See what happens when we work together?"

Brandt looked at the chaos and death and fire consuming the airbase. His stomach lurched. The cold MRE he had eaten last night spewed out on the ground before him. He stumbled off and leaned on a tree, out of sight of his men.

As he sucked in the fresh breaths of air, he gained a new appreciation for the potential of teamwork. He would work with the Americans each step of the way. Together, they would set the world ablaze.

TRIBULATION

Ricci took a swig from his canteen and let the cool water trickle down his throat. The liquid was fresh and cool and flowed readily from the nearby spring. It was one of the few comforts of the new camp they had found after abandoning the farmhouse three nights ago. Although no one liked to admit it, this new base of operations was much better than their previous one.

Although cramped and narrow, the caves provided shelter from the occasional rains. It was also well-hidden and far away from the enemy patrols. Jones had positioned a few repeaters to the south to delude the Russians into believing the insurgent group was operating well away from here. So far it had worked. The listening post set up to the north had picked up on several frustrated patrols searching the area.

The only major drawback from being here was that their supply drop was much further away.

Ricci stubbed out a cigarette on the ground and shouted again into the satellite phone. "This is Turtle! Come in! Do you read? Over."

Nothing but static.

"Damn it!" he shouted. He pulled his arm back and considered how wonderful it would feel to hurl this so-called "communications device" like a football and smash it all over the nearby rocks.

"Sir, I wouldn't do that if I were you," said Jones, in a near-panic.

"Well, what do you propose I do then?" asked Ricci. "This thing is broken. You're the communications expert!"

Jones coughed and sat down on the rock near the cave. "Satellite's not in position, sir," he said. "At least that's my guess."

"How does that even happen?" grunted Ricci. He set the phone down and took a swig from his canteen.

"Well, could be a lot of things," said Jones. "They might have moved it. Or the Russians shot it down."

Ricci choked and began coughing. "You mean this thing," he pointed to the bulky plastic phone with its long whip-like antenna, "might be out of commission for good?"

Jones lit a smoke and inhaled. "Yeah. Sure. Why not?"

"Well, in that case, we can kiss our supply train goodbye. Chopper's coming in today to drop off our supplies at the regular place. The only problem is - we're not there anymore! We'll have to get there and haul all that crap over here. That's miles away!"

Jones smirked. "It's gonna suck for you, sir."

Ricci nodded. "It's gonna suck for you too, corporal. You're on the pickup team."

***

The drop was scheduled for night. Ricci took Jones, Littlejohn, and nine of Brandt's men along to the site. The long march through the heavy woods made Ricci feel like he was back in the jungles of Southeast Asia. Out of habit, he kept the men off the paths to avoid potential ambushes. Knowing that the enemy was out there searching for them made everyone hyper-vigilant. The ground that would typically have taken a mere ninety minutes to cover took three hours. By the time they arrived near the drop zone, Ricci was tired and hot and wanted a shower.

He crouched with his team and waited for the incoming helicopter. Ricci couldn't explain it, but something was off. His stomach twisted as the worry stung deep in his brain. After a quick check with the flank and rear security teams, he went back to his position near the clearing and tried to ignore the sense of impending doom.

2100 rolled around and Jones, who wore the PRC-77 radio on his back, patted Ricci on the shoulder. He should have felt some relief at the incoming supply helicopter's signal, but nothing seemed right. He considered going back to check on the security teams then looked at his watch. No time. They would just have to move fast.

The chop of the approaching rotors bled down into the forest. As the Blackhawk slowed and dangled above the trees, the tension in Ricci's neck slackened. Though its lights were off, the helo was easily visible through his night vision goggles. It settled into a hover, the rotor wash from thirty feet above whipping all around it.

A sharp buzzing drilled through the night air. Something huge was moving towards them. Ricci craned his head to catch a glimpse of a dark bulbous object roaming the skies hundreds of feet over the trees. Cold fear shivered down along his limbs. He swiveled to the five men in his surveillance team. "Enemy helo! Get out of here! Go! Go!"

He stood just as the first rocket splashed down into the forest on the opposite side of the clearing. The dark wood lit up all around them with brilliant explosions. The wave of thunderous booms slapped at Ricci as he bolted through the forest like a frightened deer. He turned just in time to see the Blackhawk burst into a ball of white flame. The hot amber shards of wreckage plunged earthward. Ricci ran straight towards the rear security team, waving his hands for them to move. "Get out of here you big dummies!"

The clearing lit up again as the machine gun tracers from the enemy helicopter swept through the forest. Someone screamed. Ricci turned to find one of Brandt's men sitting against a felled tree, holding his jaw to his face. He ran back and grabbed the East German, dragging him forward with one arm. The injured man scraped against the undergrowth until Littlejohn wrapped an arm around the casualty's shoulder. The weight eased and Ricci resumed trudging through the bush. The surge of adrenaline was just enough to propel him from the immediate area of the carnage.

When they were finally clear of the fire and explosions and shooting, Ricci threw a hand up. "I gotta stop," he said.

Littlejohn relented and set the East German down gently against a large stone.

They examined him with their hands, checking for breathing and a heartbeat. Nothing. "Okay, he's dead," said Ricci.

Through the trees, they could barely make out the enemy helicopter's lights as it descended into a clearing less than three hundred meters away. The door on the side slid open for men to disembark. Beams of flashlights cut through the night. Littlejohn went through the dead East German's pockets looking for any papers or documents that he shouldn't have brought along.

When it was finished, Ricci performed the gruesome task of propping a white phosphorous grenade under the dead man's chin. He ran the end of a wire around the pin and held the other end in his hand. Then he ran. The wire went taut, and the grenade exploded behind Ricci and Littlejohn. Though their comrade's end had been grisly, the WP grenade had denied the Russians the opportunity to identify the corpse through East German dental records.

An hour later, they were back at base camp, sitting in Brandt's cave and explaining what had happened.

"If we don't have new supplies, we'll be hard-pressed to attack that garrison when the time comes," said the East German major.

Ricci nodded. "Well, there's plenty of supplies and plenty more helicopters," said Ricci, trying hard not to remember the kind act of the crew chief when he first arrived over here. "The bigger problem is that the garrison now has their own helicopter on call and they'll shoot down whatever gets sent over here. Then they'll chase us every time we pop our heads up."

Brandt sighed. "So we need to kill a helicopter."

"Exactly," said Ricci.

"And who might be able to do such a thing?"

Ricci waved a hand over at Littlejohn. "Here's your man."

"You've done this before?" asked Brandt.

"No," said Littlejohn.

"Are you sure you can do it?"

"No."

Brandt folded his arms. "Not exactly brimming with confidence, are we?"

"No," said Littlejohn.

JUDGEMENT

Through the night vision goggles, Littlejohn's world was awash in shades of green. In the distance, the Soviet tanks rolled northwest down Highway 187.

The domed turrets of the T-55s were easy to pick out among the smaller and boxier T-34s. The latter were older vehicles coming into service back when his father had been at war, fighting in the Pacific as a Marine. Littlejohn remembered bits and pieces of the man. Stern and silent, he was a respected fighter in the small tribe that claimed him.

Like most sons, the boy had grown up wanting to be like his father. When the opportunity arose, Littlejohn volunteered for the war in Southeast Asia, and swore to fight honorably for himself and his people. In the end, he had failed. The bombs he called in had rained burning metal death upon a village, wiping out countless innocents. It was this act which had taken him from the path of the sacred warrior. He would never be brave again - once you wandered off the path, you could never return to it. But atonement for his deeds was still within reach through great personal sacrifice. It was the only thing left for him now.

It was late August 1970.

They had told him the village near the trail had been evacuated. Without even checking for himself, he called in the air strike.

During the bomb damage assessment the next morning, he found Joe Ricci counting the corpses of the villagers. They were stacked up like cordwood - the old men on the bottom, the women in the middle, and the burnt remains of the children on top. Littlejohn took one look at the bodies and collapsed into his friend's arms, wailing and pleading for forgiveness.

At night, the charred faces of the old women and children returned to haunt him. After the war ended, he tried so hard to forget. But the silent angry faces returned each night while he lay in bed. Littlejohn begged them for forgiveness - never to be granted. The next decade was spent in a haze, talking to them through bleary nights filled with needles and pills. The letters had saved him. There were countless hours spent reading and re-reading them until the words soaked into his brain and slowly brought him back to sanity.

Now here he was, trying to find his peace in the middle of yet another war. At first, the constant threat of death and destruction was like coming home again after a long absence. But with every fresh kill, he seemed to go further from the path. Instead of going away, the faces returned every night and sometimes stayed there all night. He tossed and turned and pleaded, just like he had always done. They never answered and never forgave. How much longer could this go on?

Littlejohn hoped the big Russian helicopter would come tonight. Their loud noises drowned out the memories. The faces hated the big sounds. Could he really shoot it down?

He cradled the Stinger missile launcher in his hands. From deep in his past came the scattered broken memories of his father teaching him to fire a bow and arrow. The principles of stalking helicopters were the same as those used for hunting birds. Both acts required the same patience, steady hand, skill, and cunning.

He practiced the act in his mind over and over. Wait. Aim. Fire. The words came to him in the voice of his father. He was eight years old again, holding the bowstring taut and scanning the ocean-blue sky for his prey. When he finally spotted the quail with its wings gliding along the eddies of the desert's soft breeze, he heard his father shout the words. "Life is a memory! Live the memory!"

The arrow soared into the sky, missing the quail by inches. The bird made a mocking circle in the air before gliding off. Littlejohn looked up to see the face of his father, trying to gauge the gravity of this transgression. Instead, his emotions remained hidden behind a granite-like visage. If Maurice Littlejohn was disappointed in his son, he never said so. Someday he would hit the bird. Maybe tomorrow. And tomorrow would always come along until one day it just didn't.

He was jerked out of the memory by the crackle of the radio. Through the earpiece, he heard Brandt signal that they were finally in position. The snaking line of tanks on the highway suddenly halted. Something terrible was happening.

In the distance, a group of civilian vehicles tried to merge onto the road. One of the drivers honked. The tanks halted and, without fanfare, the line of vans and busses jolted forward into the gaps between the enemy armor.

Littlejohn lifted the headset and keyed it once, hoping Brandt would get the message and abort the mission. Instead, the East German leader spoke a single word that damned them all.

Go.

He couldn't help but look up in the sky, the pinpricks of starlight above showing as white dots through the night vision goggles. Like caged lions waiting for their daily share of meat to arrive, NATO jet fighters circled beyond the horizon. With the help of the laser designator that Brandt carried, they could strike safely from beyond the range of the enemy's air defenses.

Soon the bombs and missiles would strike the enemy tanks. Littlejohn balled his fist at the thought of the civilians being cooked alive by the fires. It was happening all over again. He keyed the radio once again. Abort. And again. And again.

For a flash of an instant, Littlejohn saw one of the faces. It was the old woman this time. Her lips were drawn tight and her eyes narrowed. He blinked and tore the goggles off.

"Abort," he said. "Civilians. Abort."

The faces flashed before his eyes. Angry. Seething. Raging faces that howled in pain and agony.

Littlejohn ran forward into the field towards Brandt's position. Sprinting through the darkness, the cold evening wind sliced through his hair as the tears streamed down his cheeks and blinded him. "Stop!" he shouted. "No!"

Halfway to the insurgents, the words poured through his earpiece. "Sparkle. Target is lit."

A brilliant flash swept in from the horizon. Littlejohn's hand shot up to shield his eyes. He saw the bones inside of it, just like looking at an X-ray.

Night turned to day and a hot screaming wind hurled him to the ground. The highway erupted in a wall of flames that reached up hundreds of feet in the air. For miles in every direction, there was only burning metal coupled with sheer unadulterated death and carnage. His face was wet as the landscape was transformed into a flaming storm. Nothing moved. Nothing survived.

Littlejohn stayed prone in the dirt and tried hard not to think of those faces. The labored breathing came closer. Someone whooped. Another man laughed. Brandt's men jogged towards him on their way to the cover of the nearby forest. Though he knew it was unwise, Littlejohn stood up as the men approached. A tracer went by his head in response. He shoved down the anger and continued waving with both hands.

Brandt ran over to him, out of breath. "What?"

"The radio. Did you hear me?" asked Littlejohn.

Brandt shrugged and looked at the ground. "…No."

Littlejohn stared down at Brandt, the anger welling up in his chest. His hand wandered towards the hilt of the long knife that hung from his belt.

"The helicopters! There's no time!" Brandt shouted. He ran for the cover of the trees, leaving Littlejohn alone in the dark.

The rotors of the Hip flapped somewhere in the distance. Littlejohn swung the Stinger up, the launch tube resting on his shoulder. A glance behind him revealed only the rough uncultivated soil of the field where he stood.

He slapped in the battery cooling unit and peered over the sights, spotting the helicopter coming in fast over the flames of the destroyed armored column. He swallowed hard, looking through the scope and listening to the high-pitched tone scream in his ear as the helicopter slid smoothly through the sky. Its spotlight cast a beam of harsh white light on the ground in front of it.

The missile's IR seeker sent out a high-pitched tone that screamed in Littlejohn's ears. The signal vibrated through his jaw-bone. His father stood behind him. The quail swept through the sky, swooping through the desert air. There was nothing left to do now but live the memory.

The missile had already fired eons ago. The helicopter had been shot down countless times precisely the same way. The men aboard it had died and lived and died all over again. It had always been this way. The universe looped around and around again like a reel of tape, with everything playing out as it was meant to be.

Littlejohn pressed the trigger, knowing the precise sequence of events that followed. The missile's glare blinded him as it soared upwards to rendezvous with its target. He turned away and shouldered the weapon before calmly walking off towards the forest.

The air behind him shuddered with an explosion and a sick high-pitched whine. As the helicopter plummeted, its warning klaxon shrieked at the sudden loss of altitude. The Hip slapped into the ground, the blades pounding at the dirt before snapping right off. After a short silent pause, the helicopter erupted in a fireball. Its detonation rippled through the land like a peal of hateful thunder.

When he arrived at the edge of the forest, Littlejohn was met by the image of his father, standing there before him as a brave decorated for battle.

Littlejohn stopped and stared. Still and unreadable - his father's face was just as he remembered it. He took a step towards him. His father faded into nothing.

As he made zigzag patterns in the forest on the way back to base camp, Littlejohn wondered if he was forgiven at last.

But that night, the villager's faces came back just as they always did. Angry and grotesque, they stared in sullen silence, mute in reply to Littlejohn's pleas.

EXODUS

Instead of closing up shop and moving out of the area as Ricci had hoped, the Russian garrison had become a parasite, living off the food supplies of the local population to support its own existence. It was the easiest answer to solving the dire supply shortages that Brandt and his men had helped to create. Ricci couldn't help but feel guilty about the situation.

The strike on Sperenberg airbase and the frequent convoy ambushes had taken their toll on the Russians. Now the civilians were paying for it. At night, he stayed awake and fought off the demons as he imagined the people in the city starving to death. Joe Ricci had promised himself that he would help these people. Now they were going hungry because of him. It didn't help that the entire team got called over to Leipzig to help liberate a bunch of POWs. The operation had been anything but smooth but the experience gained was invaluable. During the short reprieve from constant guerrilla attacks, the Russians in this area had taken the opportunity to reassert their control.

It was time to excise the cancer. The only question was whether it would be done with a scalpel or a sledgehammer.

Brandt had repeated his request for an air strike. Ricci had again refused, arguing that they needed to get the civilians out of the area first.

After that, they could practically walk into the garrison HQ, grab a ton of intel, snatch some prisoners, and wash their hands of the entire problem before sundown. Brandt reluctantly agreed to the plan on the condition that air support be available should anything go wrong in the assault. Ricci knew he couldn't push it any further. If he let Brandt off the leash, he might just go into the city and start killing everyone.

The time had come for the assault. First, Ricci needed to get the remaining civilians out of the area. He also had to help slip a Trojan horse into the garrison HQ. It was going to be a very busy day.

The cold trickle of sweat poured down the small of Joe Ricci's back as his fingers wandered over the soft C4 plastic explosives in his pocket.

He milled around among the civilians in the crowd, gathered just outside the gates of the garrison headquarters. Inside the fence, the spires of the All Saints Church and its fortress-like tower loomed over the city. Though standing shoulder-to-shoulder with the women and children and elderly, Ricci felt the invisible gulf between his own aims and those of the civilians. They were here to get a bite to eat. He was here to blow stuff up

A woman next to him held the hand of a little boy, no older than three. In a small pathetic voice, he cried and whimpered while patting at his belly and begging over and over for chocolate.

Last night, Ricci had stood among these same people and watched the same boy cry and scream. But now, Ricci guessed, the kid had no energy left for tantrums. Like everyone else here, he and his mother were slowly but surely starving.

It took great willpower not to turn around and bring back a stack of MREs from the base camp. But that would have to wait. He looked at the little boy's teary eyes and bit back the words he wanted to say. Soon. Soon I can do that for you. I'm so sorry about all this.

As the engines rumbled in the distance, the crowd came alive. Ricci was thrown off balance by a shove. He bumped hard into the toddler who stood next to him, knocking him to the ground. Ricci bent over to help him up and nodded to his scowling mother.

The first of the two trucks drove slowly down the narrow street that ran between Wittenberg's old buildings. As it approached the gate, the guards behind the fence bellowed threats that proved empty. The Russians made no move to disband the group of hungry people who had gathered before them.

Someone got on a bullhorn and urged the crowd to move back from the road. After the third shout, one of the Russians fired off a pistol. Reluctantly, the group pulled back from the gate. Unlike last night, however, no one ran away. Ricci drew a long breath and tried to shut out the looks of desperation around him.

He rehearsed the move in his mind. The trucks would stop. He would press the C4 on the underside of the rear vehicle. The timer was set for five minutes. By the time it went off, Ricci would have already shepherded the civilians far away from here.

The two trucks squealed to a halt. An officer emerged from the checkpoint and talked to the driver of the lead vehicle. As it sat there with its engine idling, the soldiers in the back smoked and shouted at the civilians.

Ricci had picked up enough basic German in the last week to guess that the young mother who stood beside him was being propositioned.

One of the men in the rear truck ripped open the top of a container. The crowd pushed and shoved and swore as it surged towards the vehicle. The soldier picked up the MREs and tossed them out into the crowd. He wore a big smile on his face, gleaming with self-satisfaction. Ricci couldn't help but hate the man. The same men who had ransacked the city for every morsel of food a few nights ago were now offering back the scraps they didn't want.

Ricci pushed his way to the front of the crowd. He sensed the garrison commander's sick strategy of keeping the civilians around the HQ to ward off potential NATO air strikes.

These people had been made dependent on the Russians to keep them around here as hostages. The worst thing about it all was that the tactic had worked well enough so far. When screwed up things become normal, normal things become screwed up.

He kept his eyes downcast as the MREs were flung past him.

Each time the soldier in the truck reached down for more, the crowd surged towards the truck's gate. Ricci pulled out the ball of plastic explosive from his pocket. His thumb wandered the surface, searching for the rough plastic buttons on the timer switch. When he finally found the right one, he waited for the crowd to move forward.

The soldier in the truck looked down and shrugged, lifting the empty box to show everyone. Ricci's heart fell as the crowd began to disperse. Looking around, he took a short sharp breath and bellowed as loud as he could, forcing an indignant howl from his mouth. The men beside him stopped and looked at each other. Ricci thought of the only real German word that came to his head. "Nein!" he shouted again.

The soldier glared down at him and gestured to the empty box. As he shook his head and sat down on the bench, the other men beside Ricci began to shout in unison. "Nein! Nein!" they cried.

The chant rippled through the crowd. Two of the mothers near the back lifted their children up in the air and began to shout along with the group. Ricci counted down the seconds in his head. The Russian in the truck heaved a sigh and stood, holding his hands up in a dramatic fashion to show off what was undoubtedly the last of the MREs meant for the civilians.

The wave of people rushed in again. Ricci joined them, barging towards the truck's rear gate and slapping the plastic explosive underneath the bumper. Pleased with himself, he retreated back with the others around him. He even managed to catch an MRE.

As he worked his way back through the crowd, the gates in front of the trucks squealed open. Ricci smiled as he heard the supply truck's engine snarl - then splutter to a stall. He turned around in horror at the sight of the civilians still standing near the target truck, talking with each other and sharing food.

His jaw clattered at the thought of the fatal series of events he had just set in motion. In a few minutes, the explosives would detonate and kill every single man, woman, and child near the vehicle. The words screamed in his head again as he looked into the eyes of the three-year-old boy who wolfed down a slice of bread. Mission abort! Now!

He looked at the MRE in his hands and then back at the truck.

He rushed back through the group of people, slamming and knocking against the others in the crowd. Curses filled his ears as he elbowed his way through them. When he arrived near the back of the truck, he flung the MRE to the ground, hoping the crowd would surge forward to it. Amidst the chaos, he would get close to the truck's rear gate and disarm the bomb. But the MRE skidded on the wet cobblestones and slipped underneath the truck, away from view. No one had noticed it. His heart fell as he looked at the civilians and the vehicle. Neither appeared to be going anywhere soon.

Could he just rush towards the truck alone and reach underneath it without arousing the suspicion of the guard in the back? He glanced at the uniformed Russian who sat there with a rifle cradled in his lap. No way.

Two of the Russian soldiers walked over near to where Ricci stood. Both pointed at him and the other men in the crowd while shouting and gesturing towards the truck. Ricci didn't need to be fluent in German or Russian to realize that they were being volunteered to push the stalled truck. He joined the other men at the back of the vehicle, grunting as he helped to shove it slowly forward through the gate. Ricci's heart skipped a beat as he considered how much time was left. Thirty seconds?

He swallowed hard and slid a palm underneath the truck's bumper, searching for the plastic explosive he had planted. Inching forward, the truck groaned as it rolled silently through the gate area. His palm brushed the little ball of C4.

Somehow, he would need to pause or turn off the timer without looking at what he was doing. The only problem was that pushing the wrong button would detonate the device. The sweat flowed down his face as his fingers danced over each of the three little bumps on the timer. He racked his brain. One button was marked OFF. The other was marked DET. There was no time! He guessed left.

His finger hovered over the button, and the truck's engine sprang to life. The clutch groaned, and the vehicle stumbled forward. Ricci stood in the street with the other men as the truck accelerated through the gates.

His legs trembled as he fought the desire to rest and catch his breath.

Ricci ran back through the dispersing crowd. "Follow me!" he shouted. "Come!"

He shoved a hand into his breast pocket and produced a dozen chocolate bars.

Before the men could lose interest, he produced several packs of cigarettes and held them up in his other hand.

The effect was electric. The crowd of more than a hundred people stumbled along after him.

"Come!" he shouted. "More! I'll show you!"

Like the Pied Piper, he led his charges away from the city center right before all hell broke loose.

ARMAGEDDON

The Stadtkirche Wittenberg was a mammoth stone structure that dominated the small city's skyline. Both of its large towers were capped by domed parapets that provided the perfect observation post for Werner Brandt. Four hundred meters away from where he stood was the All Saints Church, also known as the Castle Church.

It was built in the sixteenth century for Frederick the Wise, who had used the building as both his personal place of worship and a residence. To that end, it was heavily fortified with an intricate stonework church attached to a five-story tower. Five hundred years ago, it was a place built to withstand an attack. Today it would be used to launch one.

Brandt fished for the whistle in his pocket as he waited. Below him, the pair of Russian trucks bumbled through the gates as the flock of citizens outside the fence ambled away.

The first truck turned right and drove into the park towards the large motor pool. The driver nestled it neatly among the other vehicles. Brandt smiled as he considered the possibility of capturing the trucks. They would add a badly-needed mobile element to his insurgent force. Perhaps if they were swift enough, they could obtain one or two of the vehicles. But that would all be the icing on the cake, so to speak. The real main course was yet to be served, and it consisted of a hundred or more very dead Russians, all of their intelligence, and maybe a few captives.

He shifted his gaze to the second truck as it halted near the side of the church. The heavy double doors of the building yawned open. A pair of men shuffled out of the building. As they lifted up the first of the crates from the back of the truck, it burst apart. Debris shot out and showered down over the church and its grounds.

The plaster facade of the church slid off in places, revealing the stonework beneath. The famous wooden doors were blown off their hinges. Beneath the windows lay the scattered remnants of the stained glass windows. Despite the destruction, the church and its tower remained completely intact.

Brandt punched the wall as hard as he could. Things could not have been off to a worse start. A good commander would have aborted the attack. But there was no choice now. It was, as the Americans liked to say, now or never. He blew hard into the whistle. A pair of men on the floor below fired an automatic grenade launcher at the gate security team.

The first rounds fell long, sending plumes of smoke and dust blossoming up from the flat open ground. The Russians scattered for cover while the machine gun team fired a long stream of rounds towards Brandt's weapons team.

Finally, the grenade launcher crew adjusted its aim, raining a dozen explosive rounds down upon the checkpoint. The enemy machine gun fell silent.

With the chain-link fence obliterated by the next series of grenades, Brandt whistled twice again. A half-dozen of his men surged out of the building next to where he stood. They crossed the street in smooth little bounds. The rear elements provided cover fire while the flanks settled behind the wreckage of the gate, watching for the enemy. When the rear elements caught up to the main body, several men sprinted across the open field towards the church's front doors.

From high up in the castle church tower came the chatter of a PK machine gun. Brandt cursed as its rounds struck down a pair of his men running in the open. Over on the right flank, a BTR-60 armored personnel carrier lumbered towards the group. The turret's heavy machine gun barked. The trees near the gate where his men took cover were shredded.

The sour stench of defeat filled Brandt's nostrils and clawed at his senses as he watched his men die.

Near the trees, a puff of white smoke drifted upward like a ball of cotton. One of Brandt's men apparently had enough sense to fire a rocket at the BTR. Brandt clenched his fist as he waited for the vehicle to explode. The ground near the little armored vehicle erupted, causing it to halt. Brandt shook his head. Everything was going wrong! His first squad was pinned down and wouldn't last much longer.

He emptied a lungful of air into the whistle again. Out swept the long, angry, and shrill note. Second squad sprinted out towards the castle church's ruined gate. They poured through the fence, this time hooking right instead of running straight for the building. The BTR's turret remained fixed on the first squad's right security flank, apparently failing to notice Brandt's second squad coming directly towards it.

Brandt watched the last man on the right flank security team get cut to pieces by the BTR-60's heavy machine gun. The vehicle once again began its slow progress towards the remainder of first squad, which was now pinned and unable to move. A whiff of earth shot up near the squad's position, followed by two more flurries of fragments. Mortars. The knot tightened in his chest. His choices had been whittled down to nothing.

Should he release third squad and make the loss complete? The men had been fools to trust his leadership. He gripped the whistle tightly in his sweat-drenched palm. The cold realization came to him like a faithless lover. It was time to retreat.

He sucked in a long cool breath and jammed the metal instrument between his parched lips. Before he could release the first note, he watched his second squad perform a minor miracle. A pair of his men peppered the armored vehicle with automatic weapon fire, drawing the attention of the vehicle's gunner. Meanwhile, another couple of Brandt's soldiers approached the BTR from the rear.

When they were within range of the carrier, one of his men climbed on top of the vehicle and wrenched open the aft passenger hatch. The BTR jolted to a sudden halt. Brandt's man dropped inside. Ten seconds later, the fighter emerged from the hatch, beckoning his comrades aboard.

Brandt's arm shot up in victory, the whistle losing its perch and falling from his open mouth. "You wonderful idiots!" he screamed.

The assault was gathering momentum. The rest of second squad scrambled aboard the carrier while first squad, down to four of its original eight men, ran behind the vehicle. A few seconds later, it ambled across the open ground south of the church. A certain pride welled up within Brandt's chest. He had no children of his own, but now he knew what it felt like to watch them score a game-winning goal. He said a silent thanks to the BTR designer for making the vehicle childishly simple to drive and operate.

It was time to press the attack all the way. Brandt let out two more sharp whistle blasts, which summoned his remaining men. Third squad burst through the fence and followed fifty meters behind the main body of the advance. Brandt chewed his thumbnail as they fired back at the Russians inside the church. The rounds lashed out at the enemy, who leaned out the broken stained glass windows and sprayed fire in all directions.

Things were happening so fast now. The men were half a kilometer away - well beyond visual or verbal contact. Command at this range was impossible. His reserve was committed. There was little to do now but pray as first and second squad ran inside the church.

From a nearby rooftop, Littlejohn's sniper rifle rang out. The Russians who were caught in the open during the initial assault were strewn about the church grounds. No doubt the enemy mortar team was down there somewhere among the bodies.

Things were finally going his way. Brandt clung to the sliver of hope he had dredged up from an ocean of despair only a minute ago. The tide was turning. Now his men would be inside the church, running down its long aisle. The enemy would take cover behind the old wooden pews, but the grenades would flush them out like rats. No surrender would be accepted. No quarter would be given. The captives he promised Ricci were an utter fiction.

When all the Russians were dead, his men would grab whatever documents and intelligence they could find. Hopefully, it would be enough to placate an angry Joe Ricci.

Once that was done, both squads would go up the tower's spiral staircase, plant the explosives and then pull back. After that, they would all just melt away into the forest. The long trail of corpses would be left as their calling card. And oh, how those Russians would rue the day they ever set foot in his country. Any of them who were lucky enough to survive would tell their children of this day. The tale of woe would wind through the generations, serving as a warning to never set foot in his country ever again.

Brandt's chest tightened as he saw something big stumble out from under the trees on the far side of the park. It was hard to spot exactly what it was until he stared for a full ten seconds. His eyes adjusted to the darker shade of green, and he recognized the large bush for the combat netting that it really was.

The main gun rotated a few degrees before the tank rolled forward and sped across the open field towards the church. Its muzzle flashed. A fountain of the church castle's stonework blasted outward in chunks near the captured BTR-60. As if the driver inside suddenly woke up, the little vehicle reversed, making sharp turns as its wheels bit into the lawn. The tank paused, its turret rotating to cover the church doors.

Brandt was consumed by the horror. His two squads would run out from the church and get cut down by the tank. There was no doubt about it - this was beyond what they could handle. They had reconnoitred the church grounds for two solid nights, but the Russians had done an excellent job of concealing the T-62 that was now preparing to kill all of his men. The grenade launcher fired on the enemy tank, sending up spurts of earth near where it sat. The tank, however, was entirely immune to such fire.

Yet another T-62 wheeled out from somewhere near the motor pool. Brandt watched as 37 tons of steel death drove towards the church, cutting off third squad from the first and second squads. With his reserve committed too early, he had no more cards to play. Except for one.

He picked up the radio in his shaking hands and keyed the transmitter button. "Knight to Rook. Requesting fire support mission. Fire plan Zebra. Over."

The seconds ticked by as he watched the tanks just outside the church. The BTR swerved back among the trees that concealed third squad, which was firing madly at the armored vehicles. Brandt guessed they were trying to pull the tanks away. Their efforts bore no fruit. The T-62s sat outside like crocodiles bathing in the sun. A knot formed in Brandt's throat. Soon the jets would come and the bombs would fall. His men would die in the blast, but the tanks would go too.

The radio crackled as the response came. It was Ricci's voice, thick with barely-concealed annoyance. "Rook One. Negative. Civilians are not out of the city yet. Wait one."

"Damn you!" shouted Brandt. This American with his good intentions would be the death of them all! There was a war going on here, and the man cared only about helping the sheep to survive the inevitable slaughter. If it didn't happen today, then they would die another day. This war was consuming everyone and everything. Let the fires burn!

The first of Brandt's men rushed out of the church doors. They were cut down immediately by the machine guns of both tanks. One of the T-62s sprayed heavy machine gun fire through the windows. The other armored vehicle turned its turret towards the wide open doors and fired directly into the church with its main gun. Brandt's blood churned as he picked up the radio handset and spoke, the spittle flying as the words shot out. "Knight to Rook. My men are dying. Fire mission. Fire plan Zebra. Acknowledge."

The airstrike would consume everything it touched - the tanks, the church, the park, and even his own men. But Brandt could never concede defeat to the Russians. No matter what happened or how many deaths it took, he would prevail. On and on it would go until they finally understood. He glared at the radio and seethed.

The seconds ticked by as the church was slowly torn apart by tank gunfire. All hope of Brandt's first and second squads surviving the ordeal had gone. Finally, the single word came back to him over the radio. The voice that spoke it was low and bitter and resentful, like a hateful dirge.

"Acknowledged."

The world flashed white. A hammer struck the earth.

The wind roared like a freight train. Brandt stepped back as a wall of heat slapped his face. Even here, nearly half a kilometer away from the impact zone, the pressure wave washed over him. When he staggered forward to look out the window, his eyes registered the dark blasphemy. The church, the motor pool, and the park were gone, replaced by a black crater that scarred the planet. Other parts of the city were ablaze too. The buildings to the north were on fire, the charcoal-colored smoke blotting out the midday sun.

Brandt touched his face and felt a warm sensation on his fingertips. He drew his hand back to find it wet with his own blood. He knew he should bandage it right away, but the devastation below snared his attention. The NATO bombs had been precise enough, but their destructive power was more than he had imagined.

Amid the silence, the truth found him. He had slaughtered his own men. Like children to a father, they had trusted him with their lives. In return, he had rained down unholy fire on their heads.

Foolish or brave, the outcome had been the same. Everyone was dead. No one was the better for any of it. Brandt couldn't shake the feeling that Ricci understood something that he didn't. He sensed the answer was right in front of him, but something seemed to always block it from view.

He lifted the binoculars and cast his rueful gaze over the shattered streets. Near the edge of the gate where third squad had made its final stand, something stirred amid the naked tangle of felled trees. As he increased the magnification, he spotted the figures shuffling away from the blast site.

Eight men staggered out from the bushes, taking hesitant steps as if they were learning to walk all over again. Brandt's chest swelled as the survivors staggered towards the rubble of the church. They stood in a semi-circle, surveying the damage and smoking cigarettes while tending to their own wounds.

Brandt descended the tower and ran through the streets towards them. As he got closer, his eyes were unable to meet their gaze. They had been through hell - a fiery ordeal into which he had ordered them. He expected the worst. Maybe they would shoot him. He certainly deserved it.

He stopped short of the group of men and stood at attention, dragging his chin upwards to look at their blood-streaked faces and tattered clothes. A tense silence filled the distance between him and the men. Brandt did the only thing he could do for them.

He saluted.

With his right hand held stock-straight and brushing against his temple, he waited for one of them to just pick up their rifle, point it, and squeeze the trigger. But the shot never came. Instead, the men slapped their heels together and returned the salute.

Brandt and his men stood there for a long time. As he stepped forward to shake their hands, he spoke with the pride of a father.

"Gentlemen," he said. "We are undefeated."

CORONATION

The outskirts of the city were dotted with hundreds of half-starved refugees in makeshift tents and shelters. As the stolen BTR-60 with its bounty of American supplies backed up towards Ricci, he glanced again at the smoking crater that was once the historic city center of Wittenberg. It had only taken an instant for the NATO bombs to wreak havoc on the place. Like a drunk in a china shop, everything in its wake was unapologetically left broken and smashed.

The only consolation for Ricci was that the civilian casualties were minimal. The journey to safety had taken seemingly forever, as he urged on the very old, very young, and very sick through the city streets and away from the fighting. On the way, Ricci halted the group several times to wait for stragglers or to go back and find those who were lost or confused. His frustration became palpable. It was like herding cats.

When they finally reached the outskirts of the city, he put the call through for the air support that Brandt had demanded. Then he watched the show, expecting the precision munitions to rain down on the city. Instead of getting a pinprick air strike, a massive fuel-air explosive detonated right above the church. The explosion sucked the air out of the blast zone like a giant vacuum cleaner. An instant later, everything and everyone near the blast zone was on fire.

More than half the city had been gutted by the conflagration that raged the following day and night.

That some of Brandt's men had actually managed to survive near ground zero was no small miracle. But stranger things happened in war all the time. Ricci recalled reading first-hand accounts of the Hiroshima bombing. Some of the civilians there had managed to survive the awful nuclear blast without a scratch because of where they stood in the street.

"Bring those MREs over here," said Ricci. He waved over to one of Brandt's men, who reached into the BTR's passenger compartment and pulled out an armful of cardboard boxes. The civilians huddled in the center of the outdoor encampment, waiting for the food. He looked over at the anxious three-year-old boy and smiled, knowing the little guy would get three bland but square meals today.

Thanks to the efforts of Brandt's men and the American supplies, the town of misery and hunger was slowly being upgraded from a tragedy to merely a travesty. The military tents that Ricci had asked for had come in trickles over the past several days. A team of medics had dropped in yesterday and spent the entire day dealing with the wounded. The worst cases had been evacuated to a NATO field hospital.

The rest had afforded Ricci the rare opportunity to contact the B-team to the north, which reported that the other localized insurgencies in Saxony were gathering steam now that the Russian garrison was out of the picture. More than a dozen volunteers and deserters made their way here in the last forty-eight hours and Brandt had taken them on board. Daily broadcasts over NATO's TV and radio network celebrated Saxony's independence from the rest of East Germany and encouraged fledgling movements in other parts of the East Bloc to follow its example.

Ricci was pleased to see the momentum swinging in Brandt's favor but he had lost his youthful vigor for war and hoped to return home soon. If there was anything the past weeks had taught him, it was that he was too old to be running around in the bush like this.

Soon, he would talk to Baker and tell him to pass on word to Heath that he was done here.

He would go back to the United States, and this time he would stick with Ned. They would buy a couple of motorcycles and tour the country just like those bikers who came back from World War II and gave up on trying to fit back in. Thanks to the generosity of his current contract, he had more than enough money to retire. Ricci smiled at the thought of cruising the California coastline on a Harley. He walked over to Littlejohn, who sat on a large rock, cleaning his rifle.

"What's new?" Ricci asked. "Haven't seen you around in a while."

Littlejohn grunted. "Busy."

"You find anything out there? Radio's been pretty quiet the last couple of days. Any sign of the Russians coming back?"

Littlejohn shook his head. "No, Joe. But they're coming."

Ricci stared at him. "You sure?"

No response.

Everyone seemed to be acting so strange. Ricci shook his head and wandered over to the makeshift command tent that sat outside of the city. Brandt had hidden in there the last few days, almost as if he was a man left without any purpose. Now that the Russians were gone from here, he had no one to fight and only decisions to make about securing the gains they had made in these past days and weeks. Ricci had tried to talk to him, but he always gave back sullen answers.

Jones, meanwhile, had spent his days and nights glued to the radio. The kid had been popping pills to stay awake and was irritable to the point of insubordination at times. Every time Ricci asked for news about the war, Jones gave him the same surly look. "You don't wanna know," he would say.

It was time to let everyone know that he was leaving. Ricci swept aside the canvas and walked into the spacious tent. Brandt sat at the desk smoking, watching Jones sit at the controls of the radio.

"What's the news?" he asked Brandt.

"The East German government is offering us amnesty," he grunted.

"You gonna take it?"

Brandt shot a sour look back at him. "Never."

Ricci sat down across from the East German major and picked through the pile of butts in the ashtray. "Well, at least the Russians are gone from here. I half-expected them to send a thousand tanks our way after we wasted their garrison. Jones told me yesterday there wasn't a single Russian unit transmitting within fifty klicks of here. They're gone."

Brandt shrugged. "You don't understand," he said. "They're like cockroaches. They always come back. All that's to be done is to stamp your foot again and again as they appear."

"Well, you have some room now to start building up your operations," said Ricci. "Heath talked to me on the satphone yesterday. Says the videos they took have been a hit with the locals. You've got recruits coming your way. We'll train 'em up and get you started. How's it feel to be the King of Saxony?"

Brandt shrugged and waved the comment away. "Means nothing. Your government will have its hand in the pie. Making sure we buy your Big Macs and Coca-Cola. From one master to another."

Ricci smashed out the butt of his cigarette on the plastic tray. "Come on. You really think that?" he said.

"Maybe…," Brandt muttered.

Ricci patted Brandt on the shoulder and walked over to Jones, who sat at the radio with a concerned look on his face.

"We've got trouble," he said. "They're coming straight here. A battalion at least."

Ricci picked up the logbook and ran his eyes over the translations.

The estimated location of the motorized regiment was north of Leipzig. The logs showed numerous mentions of "Objective Alpha." He checked the map and scanned the logbook, noting that Jones had narrowed down the location of the East German combat units to Highway 2. They were close.

"How much time do we have?" he asked.

Jones looked at the map and shrugged. "No idea. They're sitting there right now getting resupplied. Could be thirty hours. Could be thirty minutes."

"Dear god," said Ricci. "They'll steamroll right over us here."

He moved the tent canvas opening to the side to look at the fragile little community. The women and children would be crushed in the onslaught. They had to move, but where and how? The idea of sending hundreds of people fleeing into the forest made little sense. Traveling with them together down a city block without being separated was nearly impossible. If they went into the dense forest, countless civilians would get lost and die. No. They had to stay together to survive. The only reasonable shelter he could think of for the civilians was back inside Wittenberg.

"Can you get us some air support over here, Jones?" he asked.

Jones shook his head. "Everything NATO has left is being re-based in France right now. There's nothing."

The answer came like a slap in the face. Ricci slammed a fist on the table. "Not again! Get those civilians across the river. We're sitting ducks out here if they come this way!"

He stepped out of the tent and ran over to Littlejohn. "East Germans are coming this way. Let's move these civilians back in there," he said. "Get them into the city. Put them in the basements, sewers…whatever cover you can find."

Littlejohn pointed to the column of smoke that covered Wittenberg. "City's on fire, Joe," he said.

Ricci nearly laughed. "I got that, Ned. But not all of it. Get these people across the river. Once everyone's across the bridge, we'll blow it."

He ran over to the mountains of supplies that sat in the guarded canvas tent. Inside were the stockpiles of MREs that he had requested be sent over here in the last of the helicopter supply drops.

Ricci swore as he rifled through piles of clothes, food, and blankets. After several minutes, he finally gave up. The C4 was completely gone. The image of dozens of tanks swarming over the bridge shot into his mind.

"We're all dead," he muttered.

Ricci ran back to the command tent where Brandt and Jones smoked cigarettes as if they were at a Paris cafe. Littlejohn walked in and sat down on the ground. The gentle patter of rain fell on the canvas tent as the four men gathered in stunned silence.

Ricci broke the quiet by announcing his plan to pull the civilians back inside the city and let the East Germans come into the town. When they arrived, Ricci would surrender and offer information in exchange for a guarantee that the people here would not be harmed.

Brandt stood up. "My men and I will fight," he announced.

Ricci jumped to his feet. "What?! You're crazy, Brandt! You won't last a minute against them. What the hell are you gonna do against a battalion? They'll waste you in ten seconds!"

"You're right," said Brandt. "Mr. Ricci, everything you said is true. Maybe you are here to protect these innocent people. But I am here to fight. That is exactly what I intend to do."

Ricci let a hot breath fall out of his mouth. What was he to do? He couldn't stop Brandt from continuing his private war. He couldn't keep the civilians here. The only safe place for them was back in Wittenberg - which Brandt and his men would turn into a war zone. He flirted with the idea of shooting Brandt and calling it a day. But the man had a point. Sure, he may have been endangering innocents but he was doing exactly what he was supposed to do. It was his country and his fight.

"Okay," said Ricci. "Here's the deal. We're going back in there with the civilians and we're setting up as far east of you as we can. You make your stand in the old town - or whatever's left of it. We'll be eight or nine city blocks from you. Keep your operations away from us. Got it, Brandt? I see your men come anywhere near us and I shoot."

Before Brandt walked away, he shot up a salute in Ricci's direction.

"Joe Ricci," said Brandt. "You are the real King of Saxony. Not me."

WRATH

Ricci stood behind the stone parapet on the roof of the old apartment building, looking out over the approaches to the city. The soft downpour had turned into heavy rain. The heavy fog of the morning had not yet lifted. He shook his head as he tried to peer through the mist, wondering if he had made the right decision to return to the city. It had been more than two hours since he had heard the reports of the approaching East German regiment, yet there had been no sign of them.

In that time, he could have field marched a hundred healthy men well out of the way of any enemy advance. They could have been ten miles from here by now. But for a few hundred refugees, such a move would have been impossible or even fatal for some. The only option had been to hide them here and hope for the best. Of course, the best would be if the East Germans didn't come at all.

Jones had tried to set up his radio again to discern their approach, but the closed terrain of the city and the poor weather had reduced the dipole antenna's range. Perhaps they had chosen another target, Ricci hoped.

He wiped the binocular's lenses again and looked over to the east where Brandt's men were no doubt preparing for all-out war. Ricci shrugged. It was his country, and he had the right to die for it in such a way. It just seemed like a shame to go out like this.

From out in the distance came the angry rumble of tank engines. Ricci looked over to Littlejohn, who was perched on the roof across the street. The wait was over.

Ricci held his breath as the fear soaked into his skin and poked at his brain and wrenched his guts around. The first of the vehicles poked its turret through the mist, promising to pay back Ricci for all his sins. A column of T-72s and BMPs rushed forward towards the bridge. They came on in a proud tight formation that spoke of discipline and experience.

As each vehicle slipped across the river, he took a silent count in his head and stopped at twenty. This was not a battalion, as Jones had estimated. It was a company - but it was still too big to fight against and win. Yet, Brandt was over there with twenty men and the odds stacked firmly against his survival. To add to the insanity of it all, the great patriot and savior of his nation was facing off against his fellow East Germans. So this was what civil war was like.

The contradictions were too numerous to contend with. The only way for Ricci to process the wilful destruction of this country by its inhabitants was through his own experiences with loss and grief. The last fifteen years of his life were filled with both. The abandonment of Ban Ngoc. The tragedy of leaving South Vietnam. Coming home and being ignored. The humiliation at work. And to top it all off, the death of his wife. Looking through the lens of his past, he could understand at least some of it. What really mattered, when everything was taken away from you, was to make someone - anyone - pay. Ricci bowed his head and said a silent prayer for Brandt.

The lead tanks rolled onto the bridge and found the minefield the hard way. Two of the T-72s stopped in their tracks as the anti-tank mines detonated. Three crew members of one of the stricken vehicles scrambled out as black heavy smoke spilled out of the hatches. The stream of East German men and vehicles continued to flow over the bridge. Another mine claimed one of the BTR-70 wheeled carriers. The explosion threw the vehicle several meters in the air. It landed on its side, a charred piece of metal wreckage.

The building where Ricci stood trembled as the battle began in earnest. The rattle of automatic fire and machine guns echoed throughout the city streets. One of the smaller buildings near the bridge collapsed under the weight of tank fire, sliding to the ground while the dust and smoke plumed above it.

Ricci glimpsed the flashes of automatic weapon fire spitting out of the upper stories of several buildings. Brandt's men simply dropped entire batches of grenades out of the windows to detonate in the street below. Despite being heavily outnumbered and out-gunned, they were giving hell to the enemy. Ricci couldn't help but feel guilty for not fighting alongside them. Was he a coward for not helping? Or was he reckless for thinking of abandoning the civilians to go over and fight?

He looked down the main road that led towards the west. Several of the enemy tanks had stopped short of the bridge, halting as if uncertain of their objective. The confusion and chaos seemed to be mounting, the net effect of it was to disperse the armor through the city's streets.

Littlejohn whistled. Ricci turned and looked where he was pointing. Coming down the street straight towards their position was a pair of BTR-70s. The .50 caliber heavy machine guns stuck out from their turrets, menacing whatever they pointed at. Ricci held his breath and wiped the rain from his face. He signaled back to Littlejohn to hold fire.

Slowly the pair of vehicles crawled forward. The commanders poked their heads up from their turret hatches. The BTRs stopped near a small intersection, and one of the East Germans craned his head to look down the street. Ricci shook his head. Why the hell didn't the officers give these guys maps?

The apartment building's front door creaked open. An old man limped out into the middle of the street, his hands held high. The commander of the lead BTR swung his PK machine gun over and fired, drumming a stream of rounds into the civilian. He crumpled to the road, the blood stains blossoming on his white shirt.

Ricci stifled a shout. Why hadn't he stayed in the basement!? His muscles tensed as the rage boiled within. He grabbed his M16 and loaded a 40mm round in the M203 launcher.

The lead BTR's rear doors rocked open and infantry dismounted while the turret-mounted machine guns peppered the stone walls of the old buildings.

Littlejohn's sniper rifle cracked. The lead BTR commander's head snapped back before his body slid down into the vehicle. Ricci lifted the grenade launcher and fired.

The explosive round slapped into the cobblestone surface of the street. A shower of steel and rock fragments whipped through the enemy infantry. Where eight young healthy soldiers had been only moments ago, there was now just a heap of shattered twisted corpses.

The rest of the men scattered, several of them running into the very apartment building upon which he stood. Ricci's gut wrenched as the East Germans burst through the doorway below. If they found the families down there, what would they do to them? Would they shoot their own countrymen? Judging from the cacophony of automatic rifle fire punctured by the odd explosions to the west, Brandt certainly had little reservations about doing so. Things were falling apart quickly. Someone needed to get down there now.

Ricci ducked down and reloaded the M203 as the enemy returned fire. The incoming rounds bit into the stone parapet. He looked over at Littlejohn, who was taking quick single shots into the street below before ducking down and moving away. The BTR's machine gun fired back, cutting chunks of nearby rock and plaster from near the roof. Ricci whistled twice long and loud over the commotion, finally garnering Littlejohn's attention. He pointed down. Littlejohn nodded and went back to looking through his sniper's scope and dialing it in, calmly taking his time as if he were at the range.

Ricci jumped up and raced towards the rooftop entrance and scrambled down the staircase. On the way down to the second-floor landing, he heard several shouts below while boots clattered on the wooden floorboards of the ground floor of the old apartment building. He crouched and raised his M16 to his shoulder.

Slowly, he approached the turn in the stairs, alert for any sign of someone coming up towards him. As his foot came down on the last step, a heavy boot fell around the corner. Ricci froze, his legs trembling as the man turned to face him. The soldier's face registered a half-second of wide-eyed terror before Ricci squeezed the trigger, sending a three-round burst into his chest. The young man dropped his rifle and tumbled down the staircase.

Ricci grabbed the man's rifle as the shouts multiplied below. His hand shot up to the smoke grenade perched on his web gear and with one smooth motion, he plucked off the pin and tossed the grenade around the corner. The smoke hissed as it released from its canister. Ricci ran back up the stairs and emerged on the rooftop. The door slammed shut behind him. With the dead East German's rifle propped against the doorknob, he went to work.

Fingers trembling, he wound the wire around the body of a grenade, trying his best not to look at the door. The knob rattled inches away from where he stood. An angry shout came from behind it. The rifle underneath the knob stood firm, refusing to be budged. A hoarse voice on the other side cursed and barked a command. The door frame shook as a rifle butt slammed into the wood.

With the knot finally tied around the grenade, Ricci pulled the pin and squeezed the safety lever. He nestled the device snug between the edge of the door frame and a wooden planter. The soldiers slammed into the door again and again. The sweat slid off Ricci's cheeks as he fastened the other end of the wire to the doorknob. With that done, he whistled over to Littlejohn and raced behind the stone chimney that poked up from the roof.

The door cracked and shuddered just before it flung open. The grenade popped upwards from the force of the door's sudden movement, releasing the safety lever. As the first two men stepped beyond the threshold, the M67 exploded at chest height, propelling hundreds of steel fragments into their bodies.

One of the men stepped over the bodies. Littlejohn raised his pistol and shot him in the mouth. Chaos erupted as the rest of the squad scattered back down the stairway, crying and shouting as they fled in panic. They sounded just like the NVA when they realized they were caught in the crossfire of an ambush. His rifle set to fully automatic, Ricci leaned over and emptied the magazine into the collection of terrified human beings.

The enemy's shouts became whimpers and groans. Ricci reloaded and walked down the stairs, picking up the rifles and pistols that the enemy had dropped on the way down. Scanning around the corners, he cleared the rest of the rooms in the apartment without finding any further traces of the enemy. Outside, the BTR-70s were already gone. Ricci wondered if they would come back again. He weighed his options as he stared down the long street.

He ran down into the back of the apartment and found the kitchen with the cellar door in the corner. The vast basement underneath served not only this apartment building but the adjacent ones. Littlejohn had even used it to hide himself and his men here on occasion when conducting reconnaissance of the Russian garrison HQ. After knocking twice, he heard the faint voice of Corporal Jones come from the other side. "Password."

Ricci grinned. "Concrete Charlie."

The bolt unlatched and the door swung open to reveal Jones standing there with a rifle. At the base of the stairs stood a large group of civilians cramped into the dimly-lit space. Several of them were crying or clinging to each other, no doubt in fright at the shooting and shouting they had just heard.

"How's the old guy get out?" asked Ricci.

Jones shrugged. "There's about a dozen doors and over a hundred people here. I can't babysit everyone."

"We need to get these people away from here," said Ricci.

Jones cleared his throat. "Sir?"

"Those East Germans might be back here any moment. When they find what we've done to their pals…"

"Sir, I'm not sure if you've noticed, but some of these people won't make it three blocks," said Jones.

Ricci gritted his teeth. "You're right. I guess we could leave the oldest ones here and take the younger ones down the road. But we got families here. I don't wanna separate them. Nah. You'll have to take them all together, Jones."

"What about the NVA?" asked Jones. Ricci halted for a moment, as his brain processed the acronym. Right. Same initials. Different bad guys. That was convenient.

"You leave that to Ned and me. We'll cover you."

"You sure?"

Ricci nodded. "No time to argue. Go."

Jones turned around and spoke in German to the huddled crowd below. Five minutes later, over a hundred civilians emerged on the street. Ricci pointed down the road and talked to the young American corporal. "Get to the next intersection and turn right. Don't stop for anything unless you have to. You'll see the road going east. Get these guys out of the city as far as you can."

Jones' eyes narrowed. "Then what?"

Ricci shrugged. "Survive. It's what we do."

RAPTURE

Ricci ran over to the side of the rooftop and looked down at the sight of a tank coming straight down the long road.

Corporal Jones stood at the head of the long line of civilians, herding the old people, children, and women along the nearby road. At the rate that they were going, the enemy tank would spot them. What happened next was anybody's guess. Perhaps the tank commander would just let them all go about their merry way. But Ricci wasn't about to gamble on it.

As the tank continued on its trajectory, Ricci glanced over to gesture at Littlejohn. His friend was nowhere in sight. Ricci removed the LAW from his pack and read the label, confirming that these things hadn't changed much in operation over the years.

He thumbed the safety off. The launcher's tube extended with a soft click. The sound brought back the memories of Ban Ngoc all those years ago - the Hmong soldier bravely firing a LAW at an approaching T-55, only for the rocket to explode uselessly against its front turret. Ricci imagined himself in his place, getting mercilessly cut down by the steel beast.

The nearby window panes shook with the tank's approach. Ricci peered down at the armored vehicle below. The shape of the turret and the pair of fuel drums attached to the back were a dead giveaway.

He was dealing with a T-72. The sour taste of fear filled his brain when he noticed the bulky metal blocks affixed to the front of the turret and hull.

Ricci glanced at the LAW and shook his head. The tank's reactive armor was specifically designed to thwart anti-tank weapons precisely like the one he held. A shot from up here would be a wasted one - and it was the only one he had left. To have even the slightest chance of damaging or knocking out the tank, he would need to hit its rear.

Three steps at a time, he raced down the stairs with the LAW tucked under his arm. He slapped hard at the brick wall at the thought of the women and kids laying dead in the street. "Move it, Jones!" he shouted.

The double doors of the apartment building swung open. Ricci stepped out in the street just as the snout of the T-72's turret slid into view. The group of civilians were in its sights, meandering in a long column down the road.

Ricci hoped the tank would roll right by him. When it passed, he would kneel and fire at it from point-blank range.

Instead, the T-72 stopped a dozen meters away in the middle of the intersection. The turret swiveled. Ricci gritted his teeth, sure that the gunner was about to fire. The T-72 needed to die right now. To get his rear shot, Ricci would need to run right past it. Impossible. The gunner or the commander would see him and a quick burst from the coax would catch him in mid-stride.

The upper half of the tank commander's body poked up from the top hatch. The Russian held the vehicle's big 12.7mm machine gun in his hands. Ricci thought of shooting the man, but such an act would probably only draw fire from the coaxial machine gun, or even worse, the tank's main gun. He scanned for any possible concealment that might allow him to get by the tank unnoticed.

A single shot rang out from back down the street. The tank commander slumped forward. Ricci turned to find its source.

The tall scrawny figure shot out from between a narrow alley and ran straight towards the tank, a grenade held in each hand. The turret stopped its pivot and the tank jerked forward.

Ricci's brain jolted his body into action. He slid out of the nook and sprinted around the tank. Each step was an insane gamble. All it would take was for someone inside the vehicle to notice him.

As he reached even with the hull side of the T-72, the coaxial machine gun spat out. Ricci commanded his legs to move faster, the adrenaline barely able to conceal the sharp ache of effort and age. When he finally reached the rear of the tank, he lunged forward and rolled.

To Ricci, the sight of the T-72's rear hull was as beautiful as a Hawaiian sunset. The twin external fuel drums gave him just the right bracketing for the LAW's sights. He aimed between the two cylinders and pushed down on the trigger.

The anti-tank rocket left its launcher with a low drum-like sound. Ricci watched it punch a hole about the size of a Coke can into the back of the tank. Seconds later, the coaxial machine gun stopped. A dark plume of smoke belched out of the breach.

Ricci lay there in the street, panting and gulping in the air. His arms and legs screamed while his lungs swallowed greedy mouthfuls of air. He dug out his service pistol and watched as two figures emerged from the burning tank. The surviving tank crew was covered in blood and smoke and filth as they clambered from their hatches and slid to the street. When they saw Ricci, their hands shot up in surrender.

Holding the pistol in his shaking hands, Ricci shouted as loud as he could. "Go! Get the hell out of here!" The men trembled and looked at each other in sheer disbelief. Ricci pointed the Model 27 up in the air and fired twice. The tank crew scattered.

Ricci closed his eyes and called out. "Ned!"

No answer.

He pulled himself up and leaned on the corpse of the T-72. The stench of leaking diesel fuel filled his nostrils. Down the street, the last of the civilians turned the corner. Ricci smiled and walked over in front of the tank. There on the road ten meters away, Ned Little-john lay unmoving.

Ricci hobbled over to him and sat, cradling his friend's head in his arms. A bright red bloodstain spread over Littlejohn's chest.

PENITENCE

Littlejohn's eyes cracked open.

Ricci's words fell out between each sob. "It's okay, Ned. Ned? Ned. Listen. It's okay," Ricci stammered. "Man, you look like hell. Let's get you out of here."

Littlejohn's burlap bag held a roll of gauze. Ricci chomped on the plastic package and ripped it open with his teeth. As he pressed the soft white cotton to his friend's chest, the bandage was soaked crimson with blood. Ned let out a garbled moan as Ricci reached in the bag again, rooting through it for more gauze.

"We'll get you out of here," he said. "You got a million dollar wound. We're going home. You and me. Enough. We've had enough of all this."

Littlejohn's hand clamped down on top of his. Ricci swallowed hard as the tears raced down his cheeks.

"You ran in front of a tank. What the hell were you thinkin'?" He pulled up Littlejohn's bloody fatigues and the shirt underneath to reveal three neat holes in his abdomen. Blood gushed out of each hole and poured out in a steady stream.

Ned coughed and spluttered. "Joe."

Ricci cursed as he pulled out more items from Littlejohn's burlap bag. "Hang on buddy," he said. "Save it for later. Let's get you up. Stand up. Let me help you."

"Joe. Stop."

"What are you talkin' about. Stop? I almost got this bleeding under control. Just another second here. Big tall sunuvagun like you got a bunch of blood inside of ya, huh?"

Ned grabbed Ricci by the collar and shook his head. The light in Littlejohn's eyes began to fade. His mouth moved, but no sound came. Ned sucked in two long breaths and wheezed out the words.

"Loc Phuong."

Ricci's heart shattered at the mention of the place. It happened right after the debacle at Ban Ngoc. Ricci couldn't get the sight and smells of the burned bodies out of his head for years. He knew Littlejohn was torn up by calling an air strike on what was supposed to be an evacuated village. Ricci tried to console his friend in the days after it happened, but he himself was still reeling from the events of the month prior. It was another failure to contend with. He should have paid more attention to the cries for help.

"Ned. Listen! That wasn't your fault. Those planes were coming in to hit it anyways. That village was crawling with VC. Nothing you could have done -".

Littlejohn coughed up a stream of blood. The noise in his throat came out as a soft growl at first.

"Hey! Stay with me!" shouted Ricci. He stood up and tried to drag his friend. After a meter, Littlejohn howled in agony. He stopped and put him back down on the cobblestone street.

"Joe. The faces. Smiling. It's okay now. Okay now."

Littlejohn brought a shaking bloody hand up to his pocket and pawed at its contents. Ricci unbuttoned the flap and pulled out the stack of envelopes inside.

Ricci took them in his trembling hands. The photo that sat on Baker's desk slipped out and fell to the street. Six smiling young faces looked back at him. They were all there - Baker, Big Al, Don, Simon, Littlejohn, and his own.

Littlejohn's eyes closed for the last time.

Ricci held his best friend and kissed the top of his head before laying him back down in the street. He sat there beside him for what seemed like hours. Hollow and numb, he trudged back inside the apartment building. In one of the rooms, he found a blanket, and gently wrapped it around Littlejohn's body. Ricci hoisted it over his shoulder and began the long trek down the street to find Jones and the civilians they had saved.

THE LAMB AT THE CENTER

Even from inside the caves, they could hear the explosions and chatter of machine gun fire. Apparently, Brandt and his men in Wittenberg had plenty of fight left in them and were unwilling to give up. That they had lasted an hour of tangling with an East German tank company was impressive and yet they had endured more than that - much more. The ordeal went on into the night as the bangs and cracks of close-in city fighting gradually slackened. Just when the dawn's light tickled the treetops of the forest, Ricci lost his own battle against exhaustion and fatigue.

When he awoke, a blissful silence had descended over the land like a warm blanket. Ricci rose from the hard ground to find a primal scene that poked at the reptilian parts of his brain. Clumps of humanity slept near the entrances of the caves, huddled together for warmth under the dark rocky shelter.

Several of the men and women stood under the waterfall and shrieked as the frigid water cleansed their bodies. Some of the refugees gathered together and shared what little food they had left while an older man taught a few of the younger ones how to set snares. Weeks ago, these people lived with modern conveniences that were considered necessities of life. Now, they were doing what humans did - they were adapting and surviving.

Jones climbed out of this canvas shelter with his hands on his hips and a cigarette dangling from his lips.

Ricci had a mind to ask him for one, but he was learning to live without this little luxury. Quitting was surprisingly easy once you set your mind to it.

"Good news," said the corporal.

"You found a laundromat?"

"Better," said Jones. "We got a ride home." The grin spread across his face then ran away again.

Ricci pointed to the satellite phone that lay on the ground. So far, it had been mostly useless. If they could get out of there, it was worth its weight in gold.

"You got someone on that thing?!"

"Baker's on the way. Right now. They're inbound in twenty."

"And our East German friends over in Wittenberg?"

Jones rubbed his temples. "I've been listening in all night to their broadcasts," he said. "That tank company pulled out of the city an hour ago."

"You think Brandt's still in there? Alive?" asked Ricci.

Jones shrugged. "Anyone else, I'd say no way. But Brandt - he's a hard man to kill."

Ricci had no quarrel with that statement.

Twenty minutes later, the Blackhawk settled down in a nearby clearing. Out stepped Baker, his face creased with concern as he marched straight toward Ricci.

"For god's sake, Ricci. You think you're some kind of prophet leading these people to the holy land?! What are these civilians doing here? Where's Brandt?"

Ricci threw up a pair of hands.

"Sit down and grab an MRE. There's plenty to explain," he said.

When the questions finally ended, Baker stood up and swept the green beret across his head to wipe off the sweat that had collected above his upper brow.

"Well, I got news for you. Frankfurt has fallen. NATO's out of West Germany - at least for now. We're setting up defenses along the French border. Things are bad. Real bad."

Ricci cast a look over at Jones, who nodded grimly at the news. So they were losing another war. It was 1975 all over again. It was so unfair.

They had come here and ripped the enemy to shreds. Despite setbacks, they had prevailed in their mission to rid this area of Russian influence. The East Germans couldn't even manage to scrape together more than a company to take back what they had lost. Yet, in the grand scheme of things, it wasn't enough to change much.

Baker drank from his canteen and offered it to Ricci, who accepted. His palette screamed in surprise as the taste of whisky washed over his tongue.

"So here's the deal," said the colonel. "Heath is halting this operation right now. He wants you guys back west to conduct guerrilla missions in Soviet-occupied West Germany. Munich. Hannover. Frankfurt. We have men and equipment waiting for you. Buried caches with supplies and weapons. Not here, though. Our helo supply line won't stretch this far east. This is the last ride out. Get on and I'll brief you on the way."

Baker turned to the helicopter pilot and gestured with his thumbs up. The rotors spun up slow. Jones raced over to his shelter and grabbed his radio and computer equipment. Ricci stood there, looking at the people around him - amazed how history repeated itself. Once again, he was being ordered to abandon a village in need.

He barely spoke their language but he had formed bonds with them in the short time they had been under his charge. This group - no larger than the population of Ban Ngoc - was surrounded by peril. Left alone to fend for themselves in the wilderness and rubbled cities, it was hard to imagine how they would survive.

He shouted at Baker. "I'll be right back! Hang on!"

The colonel tapped his watch.

Minutes later, he arrived back at the helicopter with a small group of the villagers among him - the most vulnerable stood by his side. They were the children without parents and the elderly without caregivers.

"I'm not going," said Ricci. "But they are!"

Baker folded his arms and shook his head from side to side.

Jones stepped up to the colonel. "Sir, if you don't take these people," he said. "Then I'm not going either. To hell with it."

A roll of the eyes was the only defense that Baker could offer. He jerked a thumb at the Blackhawk.

"Fine. Get them on."

Jones herded the civilians on to the chopper and climbed aboard. The rotors spun up and whipped up the grass around the clearing. The only way to communicate was by screaming at each other. Baker looked at Ricci for a long moment then leaned in close. "You sure about this?"

Ricci nodded. Baker smiled at him for the first time since they had been reunited back in the States.

Without a word, he turned and got on board then tapped the pilot's shoulder. The helicopter pitched up. Jones snapped off a salute in Ricci's direction. That was the last he ever saw of them. The helicopter sped off west and the clatter of its engines dissipated.

Alone among the men and women of Wittenberg, he found himself turning to the real issues of survival that faced them. Whatever happened, he was ready for it. Joe Ricci was finally home.

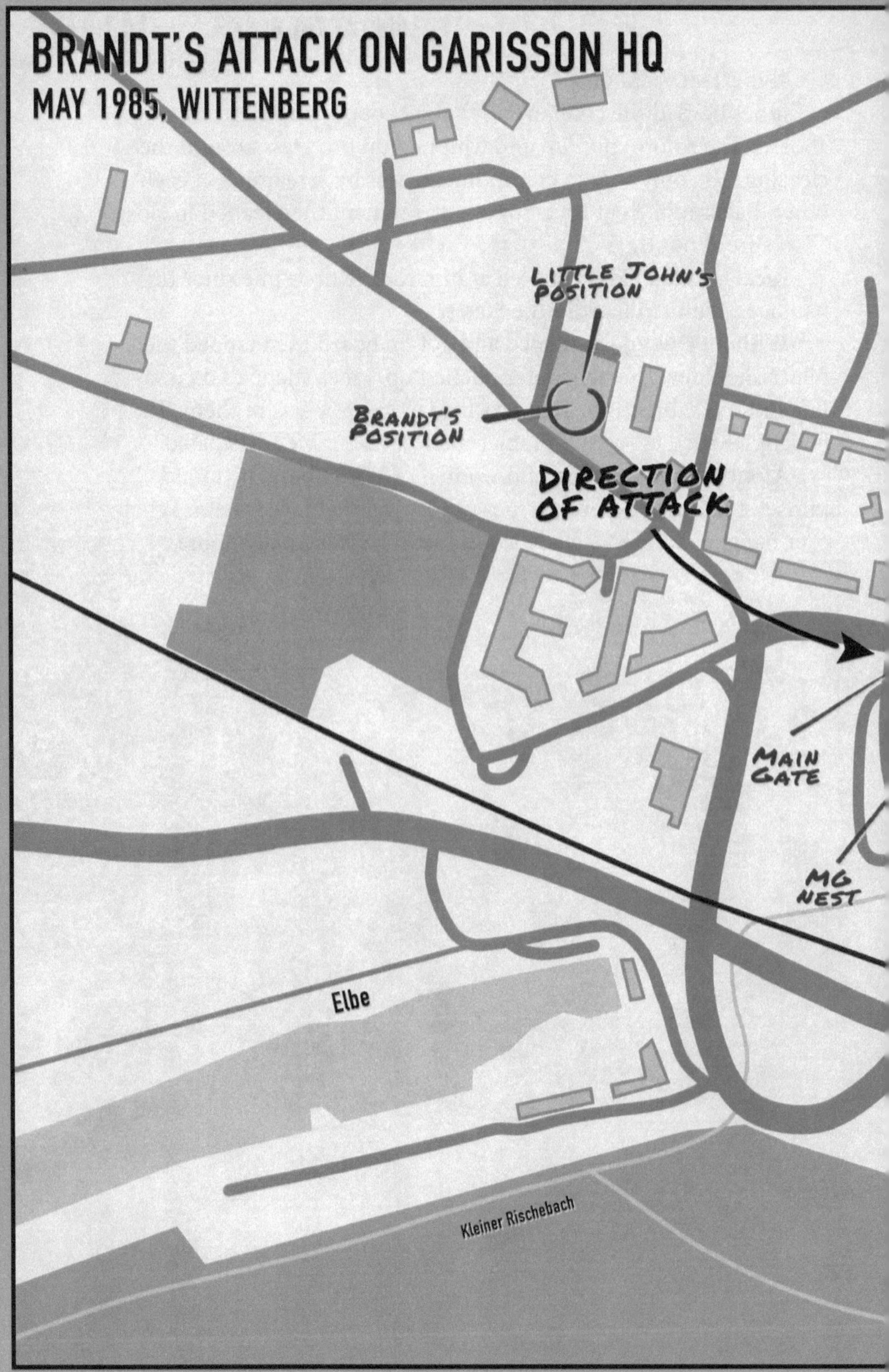

BRANDT'S ATTACK ON GARISSON HQ
MAY 1985, WITTENBERG
LITTLE JOHN'S POSITION
BRANDT'S POSITION
DIRECTION OF ATTACK
MAIN GATE
MG NEST
Elbe
Kleiner Rischebach

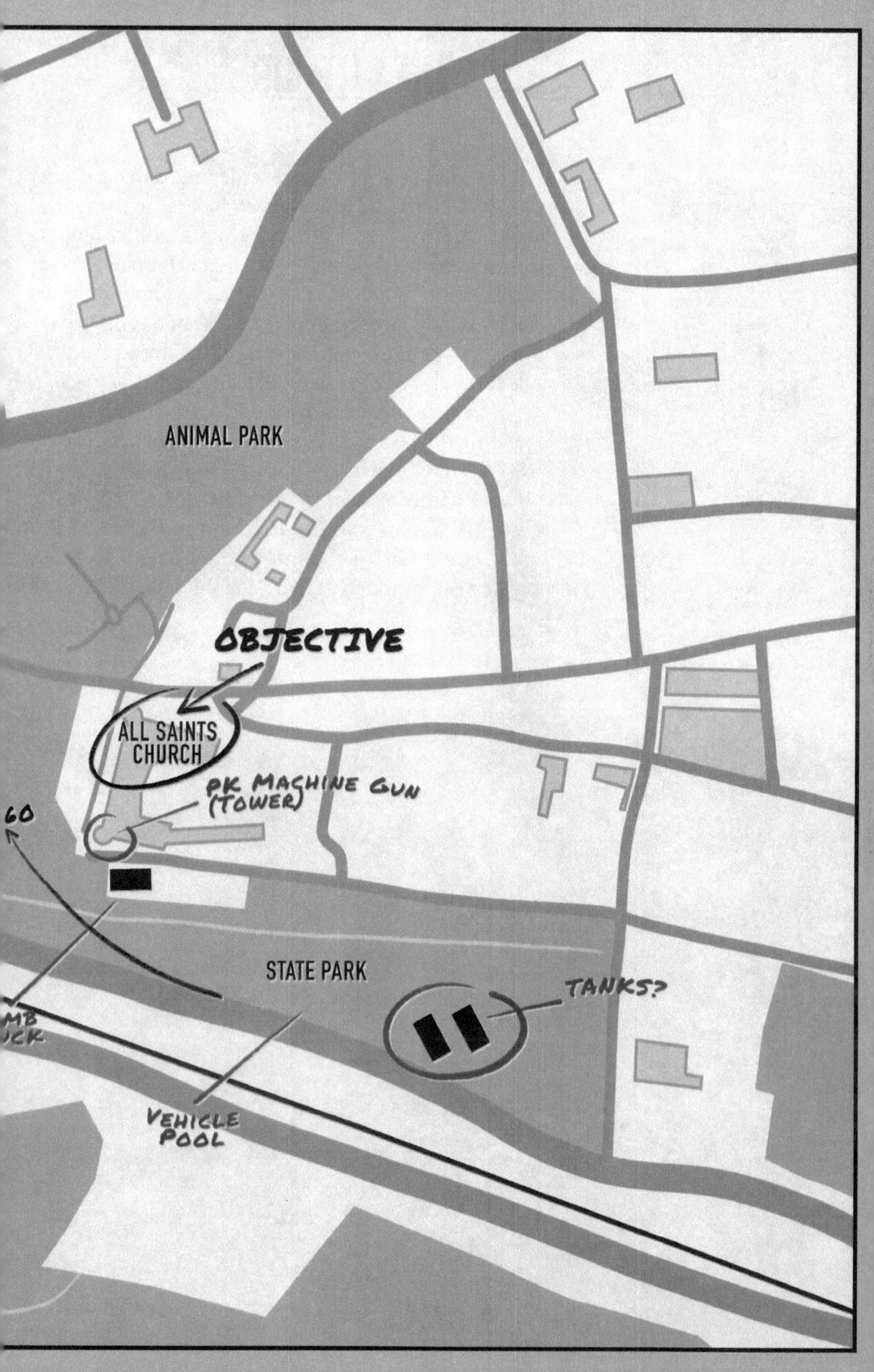

ANIMAL PARK
OBJECTIVE
ALL SAINTS CHURCH
PK MACHINE GUN (TOWER)
60
STATE PARK
TANKS?
MB
CK
VEHICLE POOL

ABOUT THE AUTHOR

Brad Smith is a freelance writer and game designer who lives in Japan. He has a keen interest in the topic of the late Cold War, which has fed his creative output. He has authored eight books set in an alternate World War III: 1985 universe. His blog can be found at: www.hexsides.com. You can also access his books on the Amazon.com store page. Several of his stories are available through Lock 'n Load Publishing.

His main interests are writing, wargaming, and spending time with his family. He recently designed "NATO Air Commander" and the soon to be released "That Others May Live" both published by Hollandspiele. Two of his favorite wargames are "Gulf Strike" and "The Korean War" from Victory Games. His gaming blog can be found at: www.hexsides.blogspot.com.

ABOUT THE EDITOR

- Hans Korting -

I have been reading books about (military) aviation history all of my life, and this way the connection with military history is easily made. Main interest is WWII, but I also enjoy reading up on and playing games about WWI, modern-era warfare, the American Civil War, Napoleonics, and more. First game ever was bought in an American book store in Amsterdam, Avalon Hill's D-Day '77. Next game was SPI's Arnhem, and a whole range of games has followed since. Putting my hands, or rather eyes, where my mouth is, I next decided to help out proofreading rulebooks. Some gaming magazines were next, like War Diary magazine. I also write about boardwargames for Ducosim's (DutchConflictSimulation) Spel! magazine, and sometimes try to write a decent article for a magazine too. Daytime job is at a small insurance broker as a claims handler.

AUDIO BOOK EDITION

- Narrated By: Preston Rosales -

Thanks for listening to the audiobook! I'm a freelancer. I love voice-overs and audiobook narrations, but i'm still new to the industry. Most of my time is spent teaching English as a second language through online platforms. I also really enjoy working on and playing video games through Unity and RPG Maker. Anything with a good story will get my attention. In my free time, I enjoy singing harmonies with my wife and playing make-believe with my two sons, ages 1 and 2. I also create T-shirt Designs and sell shirts on Amazon: I Surrender All T-shirts.

WHAT IS THE WORLD AT WAR 85 GAME SERIES

- by David Heath -

I am the Director of Operations at Lock 'n Load Publishing, where we produce both tabletop and computer games with a strategy theme. So what made us publish a book of short stories? The love of gaming. These short stories were inspired by the kind of stories friends share about games they played and the adventures they experienced while playing them. Those stories always remind me of the kind told by my Dad, his friends, and my own buddies who spent time in the service.

The idea for this book series started from a long desire to hear the stories of other gamers, and to share my love for gaming. This project became real thanks to Brad Smith, Hans Korting, Keith Tracton, and many others. Without their support this never would have happened. While talking this over it became clear we weren't the only ones who enjoyed telling and listening to gaming adventures.

This story use a number of things from our World at War 85 game series, specifically the names units and even the occasional moments inspired by game events. This added a new level to our stories and added the ability and similarity for these men to live on in each of our games.

Some of you may be wondering what the World at War 85 game series is all about. The World at War 85 (WaW85) series is a dynamic platoon-level tactical combat board game series centered on armored combat from the 1980s in a fictional World War III setting. With unparalleled artwork and a formation based game mechanic that keeps both players constantly involved, each action-packed engagement plays out cinematically. Decisions need to be made quickly. Tactical leadership is key. Unique abilities and synergies enhance effectiveness. And detailed objectives based ont he scenario layout encourages bold gameplay. There is even a Solo module for those quiet nights at home.

Platoon combat is central to WaW85, but besides Heavy Armor and Soft Armor units, we have Support Weapon such as mortars, heavy machine guns, and anti-tank guns. There are also Helicopters, faction Leaders, fixed-wing Close Air Support and an in depth suit of Artillery options, both on and off-board. Individuals such as Leaders, Special Weapons Teams, and, of course, Special Forces, complete the forces available for each side. We also have free downloadable game walkthroughs, making the game series more accessible to new players more than ever.

Whether you are a fan of 80s-era military fiction or the World War 3 setting, the WaW85 series has you covered with a variety of boxed games and expansions, including an evolving storyline to follow as you play through ear game in the series. With WaW85 the gaming never ends. It's Platoon-level tactical combat at its best!

WORLD AT WAR 85 NOVELS

The Third World War has Begun

Storming the Gap: First Strike reveals the explosive origins of the Third World War and delves into the opening salvos of the conflict between NATO and the Warsaw Pact in a world where the Cold War turns hot in 1985. This epic story is told from a range of viewpoints - through the eyes of the decision-makers in Washington as well as the tankers and infantry fighting through hills and towns of southern Germany.

Based partly on the scenarios from the smash-hit game by Lock 'n Load Publishing World At War 85, each tale is a pulse-pounding narrative of intense Armor clashes that will help determine the fate of the most valuable piece of real estate this side of the Inner German border – the Fulda Gap

As the first volume of a series that tells one version of the war's progress, First Strike can be enjoyed as a companion to the platoon-scale wargame or by casual readers as a close-up view of mechanized combat in a war that never was.

THE SECOND WAVE HAS BEEN UNLEASHED

The forces of the Warsaw Pact storm west over the Inner German Border and unleash devastation on the first days of the conflict. Among the NATO defenders of West Germany are Captain Kurt Mohr and his company of Leopard tanks. Outgunned and outnumbered, the men must conduct vital delaying operations until reinforcements can mobilize to stop the communists in their tracks.

To make matters worse, Mohr's leadership is challenged at every step by internal politics that jeopardize the mission and his men's lives. Each critical decision brings the company to the brink of tearing itself apart - posing a threat as dangerous as the enemy itself. Can Mohr keep his men together and stay alive or will his first day of war be his last?